Death 101: Extra Credit

A Cassandra Sato Mystery Book 4

Kelly Brakenhoff

Emerald Prairie Press

ISBN 9781957938011 [Paperback]

ASIN B0CBNDYGVH

Also By Kelly Brakenhoff

"This isn't a course about Death and Dying,
it's about Life and Living."
~ Dr. Julie Masters
Go Husker Nation!

Previously in the series

PREVIOUSLY IN *DEAD OF WINTER BREAK*

Previously in the Cassandra Sato series, we left off with the events of *Dead of Winter Break.* Cassandra Sato, our determined sleuth, found herself caught up in another murder mystery during what was supposed to be a peaceful Winter Break.

The story begins with the unfortunate death of her boss, Dr. Nielson, which the police deem a burglary gone wrong. With suspicions swirling, Cassandra takes it upon herself to investigate the murder and find the true culprit. As she delves deeper into the case, Cassandra uncovers surprising secrets at Morton College and unexpected connections that shed light on the motives behind the crime.

Amidst her investigation, a treacherous snowstorm hits the area, causing a tree to fall on Cassandra's house and leaving her temporarily displaced. Forced to seek shelter elsewhere, she finds herself residing in the international student dormitory while her home undergoes repairs. Cassandra encounters Sean Gill, the son of her neighbor, who happens to be in town for the holidays and a work project for the USDA.

As Cassandra continues her pursuit of justice, she becomes entangled in a dangerous situation when she is kidnapped by the unknown culprit. However, with her resilience and resourcefulness, she manages to escape which leads to a dramatic showdown at the Wahoo airport.

Throughout the ordeal, the dormitory students step up to care for Cassandra's dog, Murphy, while she is missing and recovering in the hospital. Gradually, Murphy's hostility towards Cassandra subsides, and he eventually accepts her as his new owner, forming a bond between them.

The book concludes with the Opening Convocation for the Spring Semester and the appointment of Dr. Bob Gregory as the Interim President, marking the beginning of a new chapter in Cassandra's life and setting the stage for the current installment, *Death 101: Extra Credit.*

Hawaiian Terms Glossary

Most of the Hawaiian words appearing in this series can be guessed from sentence context. If you ever get stumped, check back to this page and confirm the meaning of the word. These terms are used in everyday life and conversations in Hawai'i where Cassandra Sato was born and raised.

ALOHA: hello, goodbye, and love or affection

DA KINE: the word you use when you don't know the word, whatsit, that thing

HAOLE: a white person, a foreigner, a tourist, a person not from Hawai'i or Polynesia

HULA: a type of dance of Hawai'i

KEIKI: children

MANAPUA: Delicious food with origins from China (char siu bao). Usually sweet & sour pork wrapped in a steamed slightly sweet bun.

MUSUBI: Spam musubi is a popular food in Hawai'i and typically uses spam, rice, nori, and shoyu (soy sauce).

MANA: a sacred word from native Hawaiian culture meaning the spiritual energy of power and strength.

MAHALO: thank you, gratitude, respect

'OHANA: family

'ONO: delicious food

PAU: finished, done

TUTU: grandma

WAHINE: female or woman

RECURRING CHARACTERS WITH SPEAKING parts are listed here. There are a few extras in each story who have names, but you don't see them often enough to worry about their full biographies.

Morton College Faculty and Staff

- DR. CASSANDRA SATO: Vice President of Student Affairs

- MEG O'BRIEN: ASL Interpreter Coordinator and Cassandra's best friend

- CINDA WELLER: Counseling and Career Services Director

- MARCUS FISCHER: Vice President of Facilities and Maintenance, Cassandra's boyfriend.

- ANDY SUMMERS: Morton College Campus Security Director

- DR. SHANNON BRYANT: Professor and Chairperson for the Deaf Studies department

- DR. TERRANCE ZIMMERMAN: Biology professor and Faculty Senate Chairperson

- GIA TORRES: Political Science professor and Cassandra's friend/mentor

- DR. SIMON HARRIS: Anthropology professor and *The Three Musketeers* play director

- BOB SOUKUP: Morton College Board of Directors, owner of the Gas and Sweets

- ALAN HERSHEY: Chairman of the Morton College Board of Directors

- DR. BOB GREGORY: Interim President and former Business Office and Financial Aid Director

- DR. FRAN MORRISON: Applicant for Morton College President

- DR. GARY NIELSON: Former Morton College President
- DR. DEBORAH WINTERS: Former Interim President and Murphy the dog's original owner

Students

- LANCE ERICKSON
- SAM SOUKUP
- NATE PARKER
- DEVON MCKENZIE
- RACHEL NAGLE

Carson, Nebraska townspeople

- SHERIFF HART
- DEPUTY SCOTT TATE
- MR. & MRS. GILL: Cassandra's next door neighbors
- SEAN GILL: USDA worker, son of neighbors Mr. & Mrs. Gill
- RHONDA SOUKUP: Owner of the Sweets Bakery in the Gas and Sweets
- JACOB WELLER: Cinda's husband
- CONNOR O'BRIEN AND TONY: Meg's husband who works at the Army National Guard with Marcus Fischer on the weekends and his & Meg's son
- DEREK SWANSON: Reporter from the *Omaha Daily News*

Chapter One

CASSANDRA SATO TOOK A deep breath and surveyed the scene in front of her. Her parents were outside her house chatting away with the neighbor man across the street. The way they gestured to a large magnolia tree full of pink blooms, she guessed they were comparing gardening patterns in Nebraska to theirs at home in Hawai'i.

Her bungalow style home looked similar to the others on her quiet street. Two stories, detached one-car garage, small backyard, landscaped front yard with well-tended flower beds. The small town of Carson fit the Midwestern stereotype in almost every way.

Cassandra's dad wasn't a big talker, but her mother could strike up a conversation with anyone, willing or not, and Cassandra lost count during her childhood at how many times she'd been embarrassed by her mother's outgoing personality.

Meanwhile, her West Highland Terrier dog, Murphy, was wagging his tail excitedly at the sight of her next door neighbor's poop scooping service truck. Murphy begged to go outside, so Cassandra took him to the backyard where he ran straight to the college-aged worker who methodically walked the yard carrying a hoe-like device and a customized scoop.

The young man crouched down next to the fence where Murphy was bouncing and barking excitedly and pulled a treat from his pocket, which Murphy eagerly gobbled up.

As the man went about his job, Cassandra said, "My dog seems to recognize your truck."

"Yeah, he's run outside the past few times after I pulled up. What's his name?" He came back to the fence and held his palm low while the dog sniffed his hand.

"Murphy," said Cassandra. "Usually he comes to the office with me at Morton College, but I've been off work recently."

"I'm Nate Parker, a sophomore at the college." He poked a finger through the chain links and scratched behind Murphy's ear.

His kindness and thoughtfulness impressed her, despite not being his customer. "Let me know if you ever need a reference for your next job. You seem to take customer service seriously."

Medium height and average build, Nate's hoodie covered his hair, so she could only see his friendly face. He shrugged. "I'm good with dogs. My boss lets me fit my hours in around my other commitments, and the money helps me with rent and stuff."

"Well, thank you for being so nice to Murphy. He can be fickle about who he likes." Mostly, Murphy was touchy around her. She'd adopted him only a few months earlier, but they were still adjusting to each other.

Cassandra watched as Nate finished his job and drove away, a pang of guilt washing over her. She hadn't taken the time to get to know all her neighbors, much less the friendly young man who had been feeding her dog treats. At the same time, she felt impatient to get back to work, obsessed with climbing the academic ladder at Morton College and using her current position as Vice President of Student Affairs as a stepping stone to something bigger.

Her mother's voice broke through her thoughts. "Hey honey girl, you been staring into da sky for five minutes already. What happen?" To local Carson residents, her parents had an accent from being born and raised on Oahu, the descendants of Japanese immigrants. People called it Pidgin English or Creole, but to Cassandra it just sounded like home.

She could switch comfortably between island style casual language and formal academic discourse with ease, depending on the situation. Cassandra shook her head, trying to clear her mind. "Eh, sorry, Mom. I was just thinking about work."

"Again?" her mother sighed. "You always thinkin' about work. You need relax more."

"I have been enjoying myself," Cassandra protested. "I took time off to spend with you and Dad."

They walked around to the back door and went inside the kitchen with Murphy on their heels. Her mother grabbed a treat from the tiny pantry, and Murphy inhaled it and rushed farther into the house.

"True, true," her mother conceded. "But we still neva gone to Omaha Zoo yet. And we gotta finish Meg's baby shower project yet, too."

Her best friend Meg O'Brien was expecting her second child in a few weeks, and Cassandra would be able to play auntie to a new baby soon. Her brother and two sisters all lived back home on Oahu. One of the hardest things about moving four thousand miles away for her dream job was leaving behind her nieces and nephews.

Visiting a bunch of caged animals wasn't exactly her favorite way to spend an afternoon, but she pasted a smile on her face and nodded. "Sure, Mom. We'll see the zoo before you leave. And I got us tickets to see *The Three Musketeers* show on opening night."

"You get that hunky Marcus Fischer to come to the play, right?" Her mother gave her a pointed look. "And when you gonna settle down and have some keiki?"

Fischer had tagged along once or twice during their vacation, but meeting him at the play was a big deal. Since they were co-workers, they tended to keep their personal relationship private. Attending the play together gave her an opportunity to get dressed up and go out together as a couple for the first time with their work colleagues. Maybe she was overthinking it, but to her, taking their relationship public felt like a milestone.

Cassandra resisted the urge to roll her eyes. "Yes, I got him a ticket too. But not everyone is built for having a family, Mom."

"You and Paul wudda make beautiful babies," Mom said softly. "Sad, yah."

"True, but he's been gone six years now. My life is headed in a different direction." Cassandra had nothing new to add to the same tired conversation. "If I'm going to have a successful career, I have to make choices on where I spend my time and energy."

When her phone buzzed with a priority email notification, Cassandra was relieved for an excuse to cut short the third degree about her romantic life. But her heart sank as she read the email:

```
"We regret to inform you that your grant
application is incomplete due to budget
inconsistencies and missing references.
Please see the instructions below to revise
and resubmit your application within twenty
four hours..."
```

Cassandra's head swam with disbelief.

She and her colleague Shannon Bryant had been working on this grant application for months. In front of the full board of directors meeting in December, Cassandra had staked her reputation on loyalty to the Deaf Studies student group and their request to upgrade the campus emergency alerts to a text-based delivery system.

Cassandra needed a win on this grant.

She had only worked at Morton since August, but her time had already been filled with mayhem. Cassandra had to prove she was capable of raising funds for the college if she ever wanted to make it to the top. Her hard work and dedication would be listed in detail on her resume for when she began her hunt for prestigious presidential positions in the future. Failure was not an option.

She excused herself from her mother and rushed to her home office desk to check her laptop. Unease spread through Cassandra's chest as her eyes scanned the application pages, trying to pinpoint the problem. That's when she saw it - the budget was completely messed up, and the references page was missing.

While she waited for a response, she searched for the missing documents. Ten minutes later, she had to accept that they weren't in her local or shared folders and this wasn't something she could quickly answer from home. Finally her phone buzzed with a reply:

Shannon Bryant

What's up?

Controlling her emotions was a challenge. She added a red frown emoji for emphasis.

Cassandra

What's up is our grant wasn't accepted.

Shannon Bryant

Wait, what happened?

Cassandra

That's what I want to know. The committee says there were budget inconsistencies and missing references. Did you send in the wrong version of the proposal?

She winced at how blunt that accusation looked in text. In the months she'd known him, Shannon was a very competent professor. He cared deeply about issues affecting the Deaf community and his students.

Shannon Bryant

Of course not!

Cassandra

Well, we need to find out what happened. We put too much work into this to let it slip through our fingers.

Cassandra sighed. Shannon said he was busy at the Performing Arts Center for *The Three Musketeers* dress rehearsal, and he had a backup of the proposal saved on a thumb drive in his bag. She could stop over and pick it up.

"Change of plans," she called out to her parents. "How would you guys like to come with me to the campus? I have to meet a friend at *The Three Musketeers* dress rehearsal. It shouldn't take very long. Afterwards we can get takeout dinner from The Home Team bar."

The Performing Arts Center radiated opulence with its elaborate lobby trimmed with gilded columns and artwork that lined the walls. Crystal chandeliers illuminated the room, while workers scurried around setting up. Vases filled with fresh flowers rested on opposite ends of the corner concession stand.

Margie Gallagher waved from behind the refreshment counter, her generous curves accentuated by her apron. "Cassandra! Good to see you again!" She smiled warmly, as if seeing Cassandra made her day better too. Margie ran one of the three bars in Carson, so she knew most everyone around town.

"Mrs. Gallagher, you remember meeting my parents last week at The Home Team? I don't know where you find the time to cater this event as well as your regular work."

"We're grateful for the contract with the college," Margie shrugged, not seeming too fazed by managing two businesses at once. "You must have enjoyed the great family time together."

Cassandra smiled, but shot Margie an exasperated look. They'd been visiting for more than two weeks including her Spring Break, and while she loved spending time with her parents, she was ready to be back in her own routine.

Her mother picked up a menu from the table. "We goin' stop by your bar after this for supper."

"No need for the menu," her father said, "I'm gonna chow down another buffalo burger just like last week. We don't get that kinda thing over in Hawai'i."

"We get one good trip, yah?" her mother said. "I think we hit up all the famous tourist spots, right?"

"Tourist spots?" Margie laughed.

"Dad read online about a few American Indian historical sites and a restaurant that was featured in a Patrick Swayze movie years ago."

Her mother said, "I wen' loved Patrick in *Dirty Dancing*." She swiveled her bony hips a few times.

"I get that." Margie said, "I'm more of a *Ghost* fan."

While they spoke, Murphy snuffled around the feet of anyone within reach.

Rhonda Soukup from the Sweets Bakery had laid out her cookie creations on the concessions tabletop. Each one was carefully decorated and shaped like a fleur-de-lis.

"Are these sugar cookies?" Cassandra picked up a frosted cookie in its plastic wrapper to inspect it closer. So far everything she'd tasted from Rhonda's bakery had been a treat. "You put a lot of work into these!"

Rhonda winked, drawing attention to the wrinkles in her tanned face. "Three Musketeers themed cookies? I live for these kinds of challenges." Her hair was medium brown with a good two inches of gray showing at the roots, and she wore it pulled back into a thick ponytail. "Plus, we're fundraising for the local food bank."

Someone jostled the table displaying the cookies and several fell to the ground. Before anyone realized his intentions, Murphy pounced on one of the cookies and snarfed it down in a few large bites, crumbs littering the surrounding carpet.

Cassandra grabbed the plastic wrapper and picked up what crumbs she could. She scolded him with a finger. "Naughty boy, Murphy!"

Raising his dark brown doggie eyes to her, blue frosting clinging to the whiskers around his mouth, she swore he smiled.

"I'm so sorry, Rhonda." Cassandra said, "How much do I owe you for the cookie?"

Rhonda laughed. "No harm done. I use all-natural ingredients that shouldn't hurt your dog."

Cassandra flashed her mom a stink eye. "He knows better, but it seems he's developed a sweet tooth recently."

"No idea what you talkin' bout," Mom smiled back, completely unfazed. "Good to see you ladies again, yah."

"Why don't you and Dad come inside with me and find a seat while I talk to Shannon."

They waved goodbye to Margie and Rhonda and paraded inside, a strutting Murphy leading the way with his bushy tail wagging high.

Chapter Two

S IDE-STEPPING ROPES AND RIGGING that stretched toward the dark rafters and metal catwalks above, Cassandra wove her way through a narrow path to the side of the main stage. She had been inside the center many times, but never behind the stage where Shannon Bryant's text had suggested they meet. Cassandra rehearsed a few American Sign Language phrases in her head because Shannon was deaf, and that was his preferred language. Several months studying ASL had taught her enough for a short conversation, provided Shannon moved his hands slower than his normal speed and added gestures or texting to their exchanges.

Crew and cast members carrying equipment or props came and went, but she didn't see Shannon. Waiting in the wings between the curtains, she watched the dress rehearsal warm-ups in progress.

Cassandra's only acting experience was one starring moment as Sally in the fifth grade *Charlie Brown Christmas* pageant. Otherwise, she was clueless about the backstage magic hidden from the audience.

Peeking around the curtain, she saw a few students dressed in uniforms of black pants and t-shirts with matching play graphics on the front and "Crew" in large letters on the back. They hustled down the main aisles and handed out piles of paper programs to other students she assumed were ushers. A gap between the edge of the stage and the front row seats was filled with musicians tuning instruments.

Cassandra's eyes scanned the auditorium. Simon Harris, the anthropology professor who moonlighted as the play's director, shouted at two guys on the other side of the stage. He took his role as the rugged professor literally, evidenced by his trademark Indiana Jones style leather jacket and wire-framed glasses.

Cassandra's parents sat near the exit door with Murphy on her mother's lap. Lurking in the shadows above in a box seat was an older man wearing a worn coat and a rumpled hat. Squinting, Cassandra thought she recognized Bob Soukup, a member of the Morton College board of directors. As a local businessman, he seemed to be involved in every major project or event that happened in their small town. She'd ask someone later why he was there.

Onstage about twenty feet away, a huge wooden set constructed of two stairways with a connecting balcony took up most of the back and sides of the stage. Actors in 17th century outfits talked and laughed.

Cassandra checked her watch again and shifted her weight from foot to foot. She had been so focused on her parents' visit, she hadn't thought to ask Shannon about his role in the production. Where was he? She simply wanted to get the backup files of their grant proposal, then have dinner with her parents.

A group of actors on stage came together and began sword fighting. Clanging swords and shouts commanded everyone's attention, and the surrounding din quieted. It looked like a choreographed dance where three soldiers wearing similar leather vests, knee-high leather boots, and hats with little feathers on the sides stepped toward another line of actors dressed more like bandits with old-fashioned white shirts with puffy sleeves, scuffed boots and cloths wrapped around their heads like pirates.

When the bandits were backed against the far end of the stage, the action reversed, and the actors shouted loudly while ducking or turning to throw the soldiers off balance. The melee shuffled towards Cassandra's side of the stage, actors lunging and throwing the occasional punch between sword thrusts.

Suddenly, a high whistle blew twice, and the actors froze in place as though a football referee had stopped play on the field to call a penalty.

Shannon Bryant moved into the middle of the fighters and took one soldier by the shoulders. Turning him toward the audience, Shannon beckoned two of the bandits to come closer.

Shannon wore modern street clothes, but belted to his sides were two wooden antique pistols, and a long, thin sword dangled against his thigh.

He stepped between the actors and signed in American Sign Language. A male interpreter Cassandra hadn't noticed earlier stood off to the side and spoke the words that Shannon signed.

Guys, we've practiced this for over a month. You know the choreography. Once the action starts, if someone moves unexpectedly or forgets their steps, you have to adapt and pick up where you left off. Do not improvise!

One of the bandits pointed at a soldier. "It's not my fault. Athos there tripped into our area."

You guys are ready, Shannon continued. *Stage combat uses more space than usual so the audience can see your moves. In real fencing, you'd never make such large slashes and turns. Remember to find the rhythm of the choreography—like dancing more than actual fighting.*

The same bandit smiled, "I'd rather dance with a prettier partner, if it's all the same to you, Dr. Bryant. Athos isn't my type."

The other guys laughed, and one of the other musketeers reached up to pat Athos's cheek. "Sorry, brother. I'd dance with you, but we have to kill these dudes first."

Shannon looked skyward and rolled his eyes. He signed again. *Sometimes fencing is about second intentions.*

The students stared at him in silence.

He turned slowly, making eye contact with the actors. *Have you ever played chess?*

Heads nodded. A couple of the actors did the ASL sign for *yes.*

Winning at chess means you have to think several moves ahead. Second intentions. Fencing is the same way. You don't just slap your weapons together a couple of times. Shannon faced the soldiers. *You're the King's Musketeers. Don't become emotional, use your brain to think. Remember rapiers are for thrusting, not slashing and cutting. It's not a heavy saber.*

He pulled out his own prop weapon and demonstrated. He shifted weight gracefully from his back foot to his front as he shuffled toward an imaginary opponent.

Whatever happens, follow our training. If your guy knocks the rapier out of your hand, grab your musket instead. Or hit him with your fist. Even though it's fake stage combat, you have to think quickly, just like in a real fight. But remember, we are acting here, guys. No one wants to get hurt for real. Shannon's hand thumped on Athos's shoulder. *Except Athos. He likes a good brawl, right?*

Athos laughed and they all moved back to their original places. Shannon raised a hand high in the air then dropped it to his side to signal, *action.*

Cassandra frowned, confused by Shannon's role in the play. She had spoken to Simon Harris earlier in the semester about his side job as the director. "I'm the logical choice," Harris had told her smugly, "given my acting experience."

"Did you move here from the West Coast?" Cassandra had asked.

"I've been in a couple of movies filmed in Nebraska. Look me up on IMDB," Harris had bragged.

Cassandra was still processing the idea that Shannon was some kind of assistant director. She didn't pay much attention to the fighting that had resumed on the stairs of the set and under the balcony that stretched along the back part of the stage.

Clanging steel startled her out of her thoughts.

"Bastard!" Yelled one soldier. She wasn't a hundred percent positive, but he looked a lot like Nate, the student she'd met earlier in her backyard, scooping the neighbor's dog poo.

A second later, a bandit shouted, "Pay attention, you idiot!" He lunged aggressively, hitting the soldier's sword high, then low.

The others lowered their weapons and slowly backed away, forming a circle around the two guys, who continued stepping forward and backward while crossing blades. The musketeer thrusted and missed, then he ducked.

The bandit lost his balance and stumbled onto one knee.

Not more than ten feet away from Cassandra, the soldier rested the tip of his sword on the ground, his hair damp with sweat. His eyebrows met in a ferocious frown while he waited for the bandit to stand. "You asked for it, Sam."

Her heart thumped hard in her chest, but she stood frozen to her spot offstage.

Suddenly the bandit lurched forward and thrust at the soldier's upper arm.

The soldier yelled, "Hey!" He dropped his sword and grabbed his arm with his other hand, his chest heaving from exertion.

Cassandra gasped, shocked by the violence.

They did not appear to be acting anymore.

Shannon stepped between them and signed vigorously, *I said, use your brains!* He looked at the musketeer's arm where the white shirt-sleeve had torn, and a bloody scratch stained the fabric around the hole. He pointed at both fighters and waved them off stage. *Sam and Nate, clean up and calm down. Curtain is in 40 minutes.*

Nate and Sam had obviously let their emotions get away from them. Had there been problems during previous rehearsals? Which administrator had approved this play selection, anyway? It seemed pretty dangerous to have multiple people fighting on such a small stage area.

Originally, she had thought the play exciting and entertaining, but now she found herself worrying. She intended to grill Shannon later about the safety of this whole production.

Shannon stood just out of her reach watching the remaining actors who hopped back and forth, swords clanging, while several other fighters cheered behind them. When the action continued for several minutes and he didn't turn around, Cassandra stepped behind him and gently tapped him on the shoulder.

He jumped and spun around, a menacing grimace on his face.

Did he just growl at her?

As she looked up, she noticed the sword he held aloft over his shoulder as if he was about to strike her. She hadn't even noticed him holding the weapon before.

She yelped and covered her head with her arms.

Recognition spread across his expression, transforming from fierce to amused in an instant. *Don't you know not to sneak up behind a deaf person?* He signed, *That's in the top five rules.*

I didn't sneak up on you! You told me to come backstage. I waited for you to notice me, but you didn't. I barely touched your shoulder.

We're practicing a fight scene. Sorry, I got caught up in the moment.

Looks like you weren't the only one, she grimaced and signed, *Since when have you been a sword fighter?*

I've been fencing since college. This is a rapier, a specific kind of sword. Well, actually it's a stage prop, but you know what I mean.

My bad. I grew up reading Samurai stories, not the Musketeers. She had to fingerspell some of the words because she didn't know the ASL signs.

So you're not one of those anti-violence people?

Not as long as I get to keep my arm, she chuckled. *What's your role here, anyway?*

I'm the combat coach.

Combat coach? That was a thing? *Okay, well ... where's your bag and the grant files?*

They moved to the side of the stage near the curtain ropes and pulleys. While he fished around in a messenger bag, she peered into a nearby canvas duffel bag filled with tools. He handed her an Avengers themed thumb drive. *Look in the Telecommunications Grant folder. Our proposal was perfect. It must have been a mistake on their end.*

She shook her head. *I already looked at my copy and the budget was messed up. The references page was missing.*

No worries, he signed. *The correct version is on the thumb drive. You can just re-send it.*

This isn't a no worries kind of situation, she frowned. *We were really lucky the selection committee didn't reject it outright.*

But you said she contacted you. So just fix it.

Look, my parents are still in town for a few more days. I have a full day of meetings tomorrow. This will take time to fix it.

Shannon held up his hands to indicate backstage. *Opening night is tomorrow. I'm at practice every moment I'm not teaching. Can't it wait?*

No, it can't wait! She shook her head several times for emphasis. *They gave us a twenty-four hour window to revise and resubmit the grant package. I don't want to test their patience.*

I guess we can meet tomorrow. When will you be in the office?

Now they were getting somewhere. *I get there at six thirty.*

Shannon's eyes got huge, and his head jerked back like she'd slapped him. *Six thirty in the morning?*

No students are around. The phone doesn't ring, no one interrupts me. She smiled, *It's the best time of the day. I get so much done.*

Uh, that's because all the normal people are still in bed. If you start working on the grant at six thirty tomorrow morning, by the time I get there at eight thirty, you should have the changes made. I can double-check that the submission package is perfect before we send it.

Really? Even though she suspected he was teasing her, she took the bait. *You started all of this with your Deaf Studies advocacy class project last semester. You're the one who wanted to pressure the board to buy the text-based emergency management system. You can't even drag your butt out of bed early for a $300,000 grant?*

Shannon's dark eyes sparkled, and he flashed his full, charming smile. *But why should we both wake up at that ungodly hour if it only takes one of you to make the changes?*

Cassandra rolled her eyes. With his comical facial expressions, Shannon should be head of the theater department.

Chapter Three

T HE NEXT MORNING, CASSANDRA unlocked the main door to the Osborne Administration building at 6:45 a.m. and climbed the stairs to the third floor. In the dim hallway, someone sat against the wall, feet sticking out, head slumped forward.

Her heart thumped hard, and her steps slowed. Working here had definitely made her more creeped out by random things out of place like a homeless stranger in the building before hours. She glanced back to gauge how long it would take to make a quick reverse and escape down the stairs.

Moving two quiet steps closer, she recognized Shannon Bryant as the form in the hall. His head raised, and his eyes popped open as she approached. *You are late*, he signed and pointed to an imaginary watch on his wrist. After Bryant's big talk the afternoon before about not being a morning person, she had expected him to skip out.

But there he was, slightly rumpled, his dark wavy hair sticking out like he'd left the house without checking a mirror. He wore a puffer jacket, faded jeans, and suede boots. His dark eyebrows came together over hooded eyes, and although he looked angry, she could never tell if he was serious or teasing her.

He was a master at facial expressions.

Cassandra laughed. "Yes. But I have treats." She held up a plastic zip bag containing three breakfast cookies she'd made with her mom the previous morning. She'd gotten into a bad habit of eating too many donuts lately and was trying to be more prepared for breakfasts. These pumpkin and dark chocolate healthy "cookies" came from her sister's recipe file and seemed like an easy starting point.

Her hands were full, and she spoke in slow, clear English so he could lipread her. "See? It pays to get out of bed early."

Even though Shannon was about ten years older than her, he hopped up in one fluid, athletic motion, obviously in good shape from fencing and whatever else he did for workouts. *Let's do this!*

Within minutes, Shannon spread out his notes and laptop on the low table in front of the leather couch in her office.

But first, coffee? She signed, sliding her travel mug under the Keurig's spout to make a locally blended coffee.

He held up his Morton College travel cup. *Make mine strong*, he signed.

Cassandra set up at her desk, carefully going through each line of the budget again to make sure it was accurate and formatted correctly.

With penny-pinching Dr. Gregory in charge of the campus, there had been no hope of adding the project to the general budget, and the telecommunications grant had seemed the best way forward. Now their proposal was in jeopardy, and they had hours to respond before their request was rejected completely.

Shannon made a triumphant noise when he located the missing references page, then he got to work triple-checking their grant package again.

An hour later, Cassandra yawned dramatically as she stretched her arms towards the ceiling. She felt the hair around her ears for loose strands from her tidy bun. She checked her watch and signed, *The presidential search committee meetings start soon.*

Ready to hit submit? he signed.

She couldn't afford to lose this grant money. Before they hired a new president, she needed to position herself in the administrative hierarchy as one who followed through on her promises and could deliver funds to the college.

We thought everything was correct the last time we submitted. Her stomach still fluttered with uncertainty. *We can't afford another mistake.*

You are a perfectionist. I am a realist. We did our best. Holding his arms out at his sides, he swayed gracefully and signed, *Let it go, let it go …*

He did such a skilled imitation of Elsa from the *Frozen* movie that Cassandra couldn't keep a straight face. Even the perfectionist part of her knew time was ticking. Their request for funds to make campus more accessible to students and staff who couldn't hear the old-fashioned announcements was necessary.

She blew out a big breath. *Okay, do it.*

He clicked a few times on his laptop, paused a few seconds, then closed it with a flourish. They clinked their nearly empty coffee cups together, and she released a huge sigh of relief.

He pointed to Cassandra's desktop where she'd placed her *Three Musketeers* tickets. *You're going?*

My parents are in town, she signed, *and we're excited to see the full production.*

His face lit up with pleasure. *My daughter, Jessica, is coming tonight, too. She's sitting with the O'Briens.*

How did she not know that Shannon had a daughter? Mostly they had only worked together on brief projects, but she felt it should have come up before. And the O'Briens knew Jessica well enough to attend the play together?

"Your daughter?" Cassandra stuttered. "How … "

She and their son Tony are the same age and have been friends since they were little, he explained. *Tony signs and Jessica is deaf, so it works out well for them to play together when she's in town.*

He had so many layers. Deaf Studies professor, theater coach, ...and father? Amazing how you think you know a coworker, but then find out they have a whole other life outside of work. She enjoyed interacting with someone so different than herself. It felt like they were truly becoming friends.

One question, she signed. *Yesterday at the rehearsal. The guys who were fighting? One got cut, right? It seems like a risky idea for a college play.* She really wanted to ask more, but her ASL skills weren't ready for a complex conversation yet. She always had to use elementary level language to express her thoughts and found it frustrating to ask simple questions when—inside her head—there was more to it.

He must have sensed it or felt the same way. He signed, *No. The weapons are stage props.* Then he frowned and pulled out his phone.

His thumbs tapped the keyboard for several moments before he handed it to her to read his answer.

Nate and Sam were careless yesterday. Nate's a good kid, but Sam has shared some personal issues with me. I took care of it after they both cooled off. In fencing, sometimes we get poked which causes bruises or minor cuts and blood. It happens, but it's all part of the sport. Makes it exciting!

Cassandra tapped the microphone icon on his phone and spoke. The text appeared on the screen as she talked.

Morton College shouldn't be putting on plays that endanger the students. Did Professor Harris choose the play? Are you absolutely sure there are enough safeguards in place to ensure no one else gets hurt?

Shannon pulled on his jacket and stuffed his laptop into his canvas messenger bag. She handed the phone back to him.

He read her questions, then gave her a squinty look. He typed out,

Have you ever watched football or soccer? You can't protect the students in plastic bubble wrap and expect them to learn anything. You worry too much.

Cassandra read his answer. So much for that brief moment of camaraderie. She signed, *That's my job.*

Let me do mine, he signed. *We'll find out if our proposal was accepted soon. If you want, heck, wear an armored suit and helmet to the play. Now, I gotta take off to teach class.*

Cassandra did a big cleansing yoga breath as she watched him go, then put the tickets in her tote bag to make sure she remembered to bring them home later.

If this grant worked out, then maybe getting a new president would give her a chance to share more of the administrative burdens with a like-minded boss. Speaking of the new president, her watch timer buzzed a reminder that she was due at the meet and greet for candidate number two in five minutes. She had just enough time to fast walk over to the Library and Media Center and stop at the bathroom to check her makeup. Her first full day back at work was going to be a long one.

Chapter Four

Tugging the bottom of her suit jacket, Cassandra stepped confidently into the gathering, scanning the atrium. Morning sunshine bathed the tall indoor palms and fake ferns in the best light possible. Clustered in groups of twos or threes around tall pub tables, people rested drinks and plates while chatting. After half a semester of wrangling, the search committee had narrowed down the options for the next president to three candidates, and the on-site interviews for Number Two started today.

As a member of the search committee, this morning it was Cassandra's turn to escort the candidate, Dr. Francine Morrison, to ensure she arrived promptly to all her meetings. The jam-packed two-day itinerary hardly left time for eating or bathroom breaks.

Cassandra had learned a hard lesson last week when they'd held a similar meet-and-greet event for the first candidate. She had made a rookie mistake by mingling with the other guests and grabbing something to eat before heading across the room to greet the candidate and walk him to the building. Dr. Bob Gregory, the egotistical placeholder president of the university, had swooped in and wedged his way into her role, all but pushing her aside to walk and chat with the man instead.

But today would be different. As soon as she spotted Dr. Morrison standing near Gia Torres in front of the large floor-to-ceiling windows overlooking the quadrangular green space, Cassandra immediately beelined in their direction, determined to prove herself worthy of her responsibility.

"Dr. Morrison, welcome to Morton. I'm glad to meet you in person," she smiled while offering her hand.

They shook hands firmly as Cassandra studied Dr. Morrison up close. In their previous few conversations during the virtual interview process, Dr. Morrison had been a tiny talking head on her computer screen. Now, finally she could get a clearer impression.

Francine Morrison was no pushover. Late forties and prettier than her CV headshot, silvery blonde highlights gave her hair a polished tone. She wore loose charcoal trousers with a black blouse and cropped jacket that highlighted her toned physique, resembling someone who could take on Bruce Lee himself. Athletic but fierce.

"It's good to see you again, Dr. Sato. Please call me Fran."

Gia, the only other female leader of color on campus, and a good twenty years older than Cassandra, had become an unofficial mentor. Gia said, "I was just telling Fran about our first Women of Tomorrow conference in three weeks."

"It sounds like you've recruited an impressive lineup of speakers." Fran sipped from her coffee. "I'd like to hear more about it later this afternoon, if there's time."

Cassandra beamed with pride when Gia mentioned her accomplishments. "I'm trying my best to recruit and retain bright young women to become leaders here in Nebraska," she told them both.

Fran lowered her voice conspiratorially, "I admit I knew Nebraska was rural, but I didn't realize it was also so much flatter than South Carolina."

The two admired the view of blooming lilac and fruit trees while they talked. The Library and Media Center's atrium was the perfect venue for the continental breakfast meet and greet.

Cassandra could relate to Fran's uncertainty. Having moved to Carson from Hawai'i last summer, nothing she'd researched online had prepared her for living amidst miles of cornfields where the nearest body of water was a 20-acre recreational lake. And worse, many of the campus buildings were sorely in need of updating, as were their personnel and culture.

"I'd love to discuss it further," Cassandra said brightly. "I'm looking forward to learning about your innovative funding ideas."

If Fran could fund raise some much needed cash for Morton and be a supportive lady boss, that would be a huge relief. Although Cassandra had been disappointed last semester when a former female professor had briefly been named president.

That hadn't turned out well. At all.

For most of her higher education career, she'd reported to older men as bosses, becoming experienced in how to deal with them. Dr. Gary Nielson, the previous Morton president who had hired her, had been a unique blend of Midwestern nice, moody white guy, and well-intentioned father figure.

A few months earlier, Nielson had unexpectedly matriculated to the faculty meeting in the sky. Hence, the current search for his permanent replacement.

Soon, Fran broke away to mingle with other faculty. Cassandra poured herself a glass of ice water from the crystal pitcher and scoped out the food. Arranged on the teak sideboard, a multicolored fruit platter and delicious local danishes she had recently learned were called kolaches were set off by fresh flowers and real China. She stabbed a couple pieces of melon onto a plate, but avoided the pineapple. In her experience, Midwestern grocery pineapple never tasted like the fresh ones she was used to at home.

Cassandra recognized President Bob Gregory's grumpy, old man voice above the noisy conversations behind her. "Bob Soukup wants last week's guy. He probably promised Soukup naming rights for the weight room expansion and renovation. Soukup thinks he can buy his way into anywhere."

She had heard enough of these two Bobs and their constant quibbling. President Gregory had a lean frame and dressed with corporate taste in tailored three-piece suits and silk ties. Bob Soukup was sturdy, like a football lineman, with broad shoulders and thick wrists that could be seen through the rolled sleeves of his flannel shirt. He looked like an everyday guy whose comfortable khakis were adorned with an old leather belt.

She cautiously glanced at the Interim President – who had his head in a huddle with an unfamiliar physics professor who said, "You can bet if Soukup supports him, he's probably in, like it or not."

"Over my dead body," Dr. Gregory declared, a little too loudly.

Cassandra cringed, hoping others hadn't also overheard his remark. Gregory wasn't wrong about Soukup's influence. As one of the wealthiest men in town, Bob Soukup was on the Morton Board of Directors and a member of the search committee.

Deep frown lines on Gregory's forehead were evidence of his permanent scowl. He grumbled, "We pamper the athletes enough without fancy new weights and a smoothie machine. Nothing's ever good enough for kids these days."

Not for the first time, Cassandra wondered why a college had been his career setting of choice. Had he not realized the job required serving the needs of *college-aged* students?

Known for his penny-pinching tendencies, Dr. Gregory had pushed for completely virtual presidential interviews to save money, but the faculty complained. Cassandra had advocated the compromise solution to do the first screening interviews online, but schedule the final candidates for in-person meetings.

The physics professor precariously balanced three pastries on his small plate while he finished chewing and swallowed. His voice was softer and more pleasant. "All three candidates wouldn't have made it this far in the selection process if they didn't meet the minimum qualifications."

Her impression of the first candidate was that he looked and sounded uncannily similar to actor John Goodman in the TV series *Roseanne*, right down to the eagle-like beak and hound dog jowls.

And Mr. Goodman probably knew more about running a college.

When asked about his experience with philanthropy and cultivating donors, the man's response was straight out of a sitcom: "My daddy taught me to fish where the fish swim. The first thing I'd do is sign up me and the missus for a country club membership. When the weather is nice, I'd join the golf league, or during winter I'd play cards or whatever you folks do here for a good time. I hear it gets downright chilly though, right?"

Lost in thought, she startled a beat when Marcus Fischer leaned in and said, "Your top lip gives you away." He was so close that Cassandra could smell his sandalwood scented aftershave. Before she could answer, he pointed to his mouth and added, "It twitches when you're trying not to smile."

Cassandra felt her stomach flutter at his proximity and fought to keep a neutral face. Fischer, the VP of Facilities and Maintenance, nonchalantly poured himself some coffee. After staring into his ice-blue eyes, she backed up a step. "I was remembering that first guy who interviewed last week," Cassandra said. "Every time he answered a question, I could picture him chugging a beer at the kitchen table with his wife, Rosanne Barr!"

Fischer chuckled, too. "He had the same laugh, didn't he?"

His eyes sparkled and Cassandra couldn't help but admire his handsome face and perfectly creased dress shirt and tie.

On her other side, Faculty Senate Chair Terrence Zimmerman said, "Good morning, Cassandra ... Marcus."

Terrance was about five-foot-seven-feet tall, and had male-patterned baldness. Cassandra liked his eagerness. "Agreed. Candidate Number One lost me when he answered your question about the importance of a successful athletics program to a college," Zimmerman lowered his chin and did a fairly accurate imitation of the man's drawl, "'I'm from Alabama, son. We like to think of a successful athletics program as a lifestyle ... '"

Cassandra flashed her full smile. The three of them comprised the unofficial Under-40 voting block on the search committee. Unfortunately, they were sorely outnumbered by the Baby Boomers. Eight months into her dream job as a college administrator, she'd realized the majority of the leadership team were heavy on experience but resistant to fresh ideas. They needed more young, future focused people like Terrence Zimmerman and Marcus Fischer.

"I have high hopes for today," said Cassandra. "Attending the interviews is a lot of work, but I'm excited to finish the process and hire a new president."

"I wouldn't get your hopes up too high." Fischer continued, his expression morphing from amusement to distraction. He brushed a lock of dark brown hair off his forehead and spun the leather braided band on his left wrist around and around. When he finally met her gaze again, she thought she detected a hint of reticence in his eyes. "These interviews are kind of a farce."

Cassandra felt her smile falter. "Why do you say that?"

Fischer gave a strange answer. "This one might not be any different. She's got all the qualifications on paper, but she might not have what it takes to really engage with people in our community. It'll take more than just running a good show to make a difference."

She tried and failed to understand what he meant by his cryptic, negative tone.

Zimmerman loaded up his plate with fruit and juggled his coffee cup and portfolio simultaneously.

"Did you get any more intel on the third one next week?" Cassandra asked, trying to steer the conversation away from Fischer's gloom.

Zimmerman shook his head ruefully. "Negatory. During his virtual interviews, I felt like Number Three was almost reading off a script, but I'm hoping to see ideas that set him apart."

Fischer offered a strained smile before looking away from Cassandra's questioning gaze with a shrug. "Well, I'm sure they'll all be impressive enough."

Zimmerman nodded with a mouth full of food, then did a little finger wave before moving off to the coffee bar.

"You're still coming to see *The Three Musketeers* play with my family, right?" Cassandra said. He'd met her parents several times during their visit and had seemed fine with hanging out together.

Fischer's expression faded, replaced with a hesitant and uncomfortable look.

"You don't want to see *The Three Musketeers*, or you don't want to sit with my family?"

Although they had been seeing each other for a few months, they kept things mostly platonic while they were at work to avoid awkward interactions. Like the one happening right now.

"I love a good sword fight as much as anyone," Fischer said, "but it's the first night of my softball league. I could cancel, but ..."

Cassandra fumed that Fischer was choosing softball with a bunch of dusty, beer-swilling men over spending time with her family. She felt slighted. "Look, I need to rescue Dr. Morrison from Miss Judith," she muttered, keeping an eye on Fran across the room where the septuagenarian librarian had cornered her near the bronze bust of the college's founder. "If you're not coming, let me know, and I'll give your play ticket to someone else."

Cassandra closed in on Fran when suddenly Dr. Gregory intercepted her path and placed his giant hand on Fran's shoulder. "Dr. Morrison, let's head over to your interview together. We both need to shake a leg before you face the firing squad, righto?"

First of all, who said *shake a leg* anymore? And second, why was Gregory inserting himself where he didn't belong? Again.

Gregory practically dragged Fran away as they made their way out of the atrium. Outmaneuvered, Cassandra gritted her teeth. It wasn't the first time her small stature had enabled fossils like Gregory to overlook her. The soon-to-be-retired interim president with the permanence of a cockroach had no power when it came to hiring, yet called the shots as if he did.

"What's your game, old man?" Cassandra murmured.

"To be honest, we all can't wait to see the back of Gregory, although you didn't hear that from me," Zimmerman said in a conspiratorial whisper.

Cassandra whirled around in surprise; she hadn't even noticed he'd moved next to her or overheard what she said. Zimmerman made a gesture as if locking his lips, then throwing away an imaginary key.

Cassandra didn't reach the position of Vice President of Student Affairs at such a young age by letting her bosses' antics distract her. She knew she needed more experience before she could reach the top, so she mentally stored these infuriating moments for future use. She was determined to be the one at the head of the table someday, and timing was everything in the cutthroat world of academia.

She forced a fake half-smile. "Let's find Marcus and get to the interview before our team makes a colossal mess of it, okay?"

Chapter Five

C ASSANDRA LEANED IN CLOSE and spoke quietly to Gia Torres. "I know we should be unbiased, but I think Fran's much more qualified than the John Goodman doppelgänger. She was a former Army officer, former high school teacher, former senator's page."

A political science professor, Gia Torres had more life experience than Cassandra, but had only been at Morton for a few years. She loved colorful fashion and accessories, and today she rocked a leopard print shirt and fuchsia cardigan.

"That's a lot of former jobs," Gia said skeptically. "Do we think she'll stick around long enough here to make the long-term changes we need?"

As Cassandra drummed her fingers on the armrests of the chair, the boardroom filled with hushed conversations as everyone waited for Fran Morrison's interview to begin. A semester at Morton College had opened Cassandra's eyes to their dismal enrollment situation, and she was filled with determination to be part of the solution. Carson was small and rural, so it took creativity to attract students from different cultures and backgrounds.

"It's about time we had a president who sees the world from a woman's viewpoint," Cassandra murmured, "but she needs to focus on bringing in donations and research dollars, too. Our so-called temporary budget freeze has lasted for months. I still don't have an assistant."

As soon as Cassandra started the job in August, the board instituted a hiring freeze, so replacing the retired administrative assistant who left just one month into Cassandra's tenure was a complete no-go.

"We can't continue this budget-cutting cycle. It's like death by a thousand paper cuts." Gia frowned. "Those student workers are still running your office?"

For months, Cassandra had watched in bemusement as inexperienced students bungled tasks more suitable for a professional full-time staffer. Cassandra laughed. "If temporary means eight months, then yes! Don't get me wrong, I love the students and they can be hilarious, but I'd like to focus on other things besides correcting their errors and re-training them."

After the Student Affairs office became the focus of negative attention from both the media and community, all responsibility for day-to-day operations had landed squarely on her shoulders.

Interim President Bob Gregory and she had clashed over the budget and his archaic views on practically every social justice issue. In a few months, Gregory would be gone, and she had every intention of making sure his replacement followed through with some long-awaited changes.

"I need this interview to go well," Cassandra said. "Convincing the geezers will be the hardest part."

Other than her, Fischer, and Zimmerman, the rest of the committee members were focused on deciding whether they should sign up for Medicare Part D, not how to upgrade the college's social media strategy.

"Now, I'll admit you're a lot closer in age to the students than I am," said Gia, "but I'd like to think I still have a few words of wisdom before I'm toes up."

"*You* aren't a geezer," Cassandra assured Gia. "And your wisdom will be one of the major attractions at the conference next month. Young women need good role models like you to show us the way to the top of our fields."

Gia smiled kindly. "Just don't focus on the future so much that you miss the journey." Gia gently squeezed Cassandra's arm. "What can you learn here, *today*? In *this* meeting?"

That was the closest Gia had ever come to chastising Cassandra, and even though she had only meant the comment in jest, it still stung. Cassandra felt dumb for the geezer remark. For someone who could normally be considered the smartest person in the room, she felt a huge slap to her ego and murmured more humbly, "Point taken."

To cover for her discomfort at being corrected, Cassandra arranged her interview packet on the table in front of her and smiled at Fischer sitting two seats away. She needn't have bothered because he stared at Fran Morrison like she was a chocolate frosted donut. Cassandra's smile faded, and she did a quick back-and-forth glance between them, but Fran's attention was on working the room at large, not zeroed in on one face.

After the formal greetings and handshakes, everyone sat, and Terrance Zimmerman read the introductory statement. Cassandra asked the first question: the general "tell us why you're interested in this position" softball question.

Fran rattled off a verbatim section of her curriculum vitae before Bob Soukup, the board of director's representative, asked the second question: "What is the role of the president and the board of directors in the curriculum development process?"

This was a loaded question, and her answer was important. Slowly Cassandra looked around the large teak table, judging the committee members' body language. Most everyone had pleasant poker expressions on their faces. Encouraging without being overtly happy.

"We hire talented faculty that are experts in their field of study," Fran began. Her posture was so straight she could have been wearing a brace under her clothes. Her voice held no hint of a Charleston accent.

She continued, "We ensure everyone has access to our institution's mission and guiding principles. When faculty develop their curriculum, we trust them to collaborate with others, reflect our goals of educating students, and present content in effective and engaging ways. The president and board of directors are charged with maintaining and growing our faculty to offer relevant and meaningful curriculum to help guide our next generation."

Cassandra smiled at the excellent answer, certain that Fran Morrison was the perfect fit for the job. Perhaps the geezers would easily be convinced.

Dr. Gary Nielson's face flickered in Cassandra's memory again. As her friend Cinda used to say, Nielson was about as sharp as a bowling ball, bless his heart, but he truly cared about the students and community. Since August, Cassandra had watched presidents and interim presidents come and go, and finding someone who would stay in the job was beginning to feel like filling the Defense Against the Dark Arts position at Hogwarts.

Next, it was Gia Torres's turn. She flipped a page in the interview packet and adjusted her stylish purple reading glasses before asking, "What is the most challenging part of budgeting for you? What are your thoughts on deficit financing and deficit spending?"

Momentarily, Cassandra flashed back to the previous week when the first joker had answered the same question by saying that a budget is just a bunch of columns on a spreadsheet.

Thank goodness Fran gave an example from her time as a military officer in Iraq. It proved she could manage multiple accounts of money and think quickly under pressure.

Bob Soukup lounged across the table from Cassandra, his open file before him and his usual scowl on his face. He was a tough person to read. Fischer, though, was hunched over his journal, scribbling furiously, sparing no one a glance.

For several months, Cassandra and Fischer had attended weekly admin team meetings, and in that time, she'd come to appreciate his neatness and calm professionalism. Now he exuded nervous energy, sweat forming on his brow.

Moments later, it was his turn to ask a question.

Silence lasted several long heartbeats after Fran's previous response. The committee members all knew the order for the interview questions. The script was the same so all candidates had the same format, the same questions, and theoretically the same opportunity to perform during the interview.

Although from firsthand experience, Cassandra knew "all the same" was deceptive. All things were never equal when it came to academic administrator jobs.

An uncomfortable silence fell as everyone waited. Heads slowly turned toward Fischer, and Terrance coughed into his hand. Finally,

Fischer cleared his throat, "Dr. Morrison," he croaked like a nervous teenager, "what do you see as your greatest challenge, and how would you overcome that challenge in order to excel at Morton in the role as president?"

Cassandra noticed something peculiar. When Fischer finished the question, Fran touched her hair and raised her left eyebrow as though he'd said something ironic.

Fischer finally put down his pen and stared at Fran while she gave a brief example of working with donors. When he asked a follow-up question, Fran's face creased into a relaxed smile, like she was talking to an old friend. His cheeks actually flushed and when he leaned forward, it seemed to Cassandra like they'd both forgotten where they were.

Nerves jangling, Cassandra felt a stab of jealousy as she watched Fischer and Fran together. She searched her memory for any time Fischer had mentioned knowing Fran Morrison before now. As a search committee member, he had an obligation to report any potential conflicts of interest, and as far as she knew, there was nothing about them on record. The whole situation made Cassandra want to holler. With all the interviews, the grant proposal, and now this strange chemistry between Fischer and Fran, it felt like too much.

Within a few more minutes, the interview was complete and everyone appeared back to normal, although Fischer still seemed uncomfortable.

Terrance reminded everyone, "Dr. Morrison's lecture in front of the faculty and staff begins at 10:00 a.m. sharp tomorrow, with the stakeholder luncheon immediately following. See you all then."

Putting on a false smile, Cassandra joined the chorus murmuring, "thanks for coming today," before quickly leaving the room.

As she walked alone down the hallway, Cassandra was still certain Fran was their top pick. But why had Fischer acted so strangely during the interview?

Had his past in Iraq created a bond between him and Fran, one which he couldn't ignore? Cassandra had been trying to move on from Paul by focusing on her career instead. She tried to remind herself that she and Fischer had agreed to take things slow—they hadn't even discussed a future together. She wanted to build a legacy of success by focusing solely on her career, even if it meant having to jump through endless hoops and not staying in one job for more than a few years.

"What time should I meet you at the play tonight?" Fischer's voice came from behind her.

Cassandra slowed and turned around, surprised to see he'd followed her out. "I thought you had softball? Maybe you'll grab a brew with our new president after the game?"

Fischer's eyes narrowed, and his cheeks flushed slightly. "What's that supposed to mean?"

Cassandra smirked. "You hit it off with Fran Morrison so well, I figured you'd invite her to your game."

"You don't know what you're talking about." Fischer shoved his hands into his pockets and stared at Cassandra for a heartbeat or two. "I asked Bob Gregory to appoint someone else on the search committee. I hate these interviews. Transcribing every word the interviewee says as fast as possible. Asking dumb questions that have nothing to do with real life." He fidgeted with his tie. "Wearing fancy clothes to look the part. Gregory ordered me to be on the committee."

"You don't want to be on the committee because it's boring and you have to dress up? Really?" Cassandra said, incredulous.

"You're annoying." He stepped closer and she could feel the tension in the air between them. "You know that?"

"I've been told."

Fischer opened and closed his mouth several times before finally shaking his head. "We aren't talking about this," he muttered.

That was twice he had put her off regarding his behavior around Fran. She didn't think she was imagining their chemistry. "Fine. The play starts at seven."

"Great. See you then." Fischer mumbled, already walking away.

"Hey! You never said what time we were meeting!" Cassandra called out after him.

"Six-thirty at the theater," Fischer shouted back over his shoulder before disappearing around a corner.

Cassandra had overreacted, but she couldn't help feeling a little hurt. Though neither of them had raised their voices, it felt like they were fighting.

Chapter Six

"LOOK WHO IT IS, the Queen of Doom," Rachel Nagle remarked.

Hearing those words as she entered the Student Affairs outer office suite made Cassandra swerve abruptly to the reception desk. Apparently, the student workers had gotten up to another interesting conversation during her absence.

"You aren't talking about me?" Cassandra asked warily. Rachel shrugged slightly. Her long, light brown hair cascaded down her left shoulder and framed her face.

Devon MacKenzie, another student worker, explained from his seat beside the reception desk. "We're all taking the Death 101 class, and today we learned about the Blood Countess, the most famous female serial killer. So, ya know ...we thought of you." He was tall with blond hair and obviously spent a lot of time weight training because his fitted shirtsleeves were snug on his biceps.

Since the distance between learning about serial killers in a Death 101 class and herself was not any form of a straight line, she made a heavy sigh. "Excuse me?"

Devon waved his hands like he was erasing his previous statement. "No one said *you* were a serial killer. Just more of a ...bad luck charm."

Cassandra rolled her eyes as she realized Devon and the other students were teasing her affectionately. And again, she loved them all dearly. But maybe they had a point. Ever since she started working at Morton, strange things from fire alarms in the library to mysterious deaths *had* happened.

Devon's phone beeped loudly from his pants pocket. He said, "Hey Rachel, we gotta head out if we're going to finish homework and eat before the play tonight." He turned to Cassandra, "My roommates Sam and Nate are performing in *The Three Musketeers* and got me free tickets. I can't wait for the fight scenes. They've been coming home for weeks with bruises from fencing practice."

"Sam and Nate are your roommates?" Cassandra crossed her arms in front of her chest. "I saw them get into it yesterday at the dress rehearsal. No one should get hurt from acting!" She still had misgivings about the violence level of the production, even though Shannon said it was normal.

But Devon hardly seemed to notice, chattering excitedly about attending the family and friends afterparty for the official opening night show.

"Okay, give me a minute." Rachel started tidying the desk but kept talking about the Death 101 class. "After the serial killers, we talked about ghosts. Dr. Harris told us the Edgerton Science building has the most ghosts on campus. He even published a book about local paranormal activities."

Simon Harris was an arrogant jerk in Cassandra's limited experience. He dressed like Indiana Jones minus the charm and seemed to relish conflict among the faculty and staff. The students loved him, though. Especially the female students.

"Oh, for crying out loud." Cassandra muttered. She retrieved her large pashmina from the coat stand and wrapped it around her shoulders. She wanted to get home early today too. "Dr. Harris teaches anthropology, not forensic science."

"A lot of bad luck stuff has happened since you got here. Like what about Dr. Winters and Dr. Nielson?" Devon persisted, "You knew them."

"The office is cursed," Rachel declared solemnly.

Cassandra raised an eyebrow. "Both were tragic events, yes. But the Student Affairs department is *not* cursed." She went into her office to switch out her shoes, wondering if everyone in the office was playing some sort of game to try to freak her out.

"We love Death 101," Rachel said. "It's so dark, right? We got an assignment this week that we have to write a goodbye letter to someone or something we've lost. Later we'll plan our own funerals. Pick the casket or urn, choose the tunes. It's kinda eye-opening, you know? I mean, at this age, we don't usually think about stuff like that, but the discussions we have are actually really interesting."

Although only a decade or so older than them, she had knowledge of and sadness for things that people her age should never have to understand. Six years ago, when her fiancé Paul passed away without warning, it had completely changed her trajectory. All she could do for years was learn how to cope with it. "That is dark, Rachel. And I'm surprised Dr. Harris teaches that course."

"He said studying dusty skeletons and lost cultures gets old sometimes, and he likes talking about life and living for a change," Devon said.

Bridget, another student who had been quietly working at another desk piped in, "He also said chicks dig rugged masculinity and adventure."

Now that sounded more like the Simon Harris Cassandra knew. Rachel fake-swooned, and Devon chuckled as he flexed his muscles.

"On that note, I'm out of here too. See you both tonight," Cassandra announced and started walking home.

The spring temperature was in the mid-60's. Along the four residential blocks leading to her house, Cassandra's thoughts returned to the roadblocks she'd encountered since moving to Carson and the Death 101 homework about writing a letter to a deceased loved one.

She could still picture Paul's tiny apartment in Manoa, smiling as she recalled their epic cribbage matches at the little table by the window. Paul had loved her despite her quirks. Like her tendency to reorganize his pantry or aligning his shoes in perfect rows outside his front door. When they had been seniors in college, their life together seemed so mapped out: grad school, marriage, children. She was so eager to have the life they had planned together. Grad school came with a new career plan for Cassandra; higher education administration in order to help as many people as she could.

But in one horrible week, all of that changed when Paul passed away. The tears threatened to overtake her, but Cassandra lifted her gaze to the cloudless blue sky waiting for them to evaporate—if not for herself then for the sake of her makeup.

In moments of sadness and longing, she would rummage through old photos and trinkets from their past, wishing she could turn back time even though she knew it wasn't possible. And while she held onto her memories like a security blanket, they seemed to tether her instead to the past, preventing her from searching for a new future.

As much as she tried to keep busy to avoid her grief, she still hadn't been able to say a proper goodbye to him or even to the version of herself that existed with him.

Could writing a heart-felt goodbye letter help her move on from the past and trust the future?

The questions lingered in the air around her like an unanswered prayer, but today she had hopeful plans. Baby shower preparations, followed by a theater night with mom, dad, and Fischer.

Today she refused to give into nostalgia for the past. She wasn't cursed or the Queen of Doom! She could choose to become the Queen of Fun and ready to jump right into the night ahead of her!

Chapter Seven

"**S**IT DOWN AND EAT like a normal person," Cassandra's mom called from the top of the stairs into the basement where Cassandra was sewing. "I made your favorites."

A few minutes later, Cassandra entered the kitchen, where the air was thick with the smell of greasy fried chicken. "I finished the top of the baby quilt. All that's left is the batting and attaching the back, but it will have to wait." Cassandra folded the project for Meg's baby and set it aside on her bedroom chair. "We need to hurry. I told Marcus Fischer we'd meet in the lobby before the show starts."

Besides, fried chicken and macaroni salad were not *her* favorites. They were her younger sister's. Mom often confused her three daughters and their preferences, although she'd never admit it. Cassandra knew better than to complain out loud.

Tonight, all she wanted was to show her parents an amazing production put on by the students in her office, her friend Shannon Bryant, and the cast of *The Three Musketeers*. Although Carson was like a speck compared to Honolulu, she wanted her parents to experience the small town's version of a cultural experience. Topping off their visit with a delightful night out where the only drama was onstage would be the perfect way for them to go back home with happy memories of their daughter in Nebraska.

"Dad, thanks for scraping the ice off my car's windshield this morning. You must've woken up early. You didn't have to do that."

Despite being almost springtime, the chilly Nebraska nights still managed to turn every vehicle's windshield into an icy master-piece.

Adulting was hard. Her dad's minor act of kindness reminded Cassandra how much they had done for her while growing up in Hawai'i. She thought she had earned everything on her own, but looking back now, she realized it wouldn't have been possible without a loving family behind her. No matter how far away she moved, she could never forget the importance of having a supportive family.

Cassandra quickly threw on the dress that had magically appeared in her browser search feed earlier that week. She couldn't resist the impulse to buy because it looked like something straight from her closet. With just three clicks, she got herself a complete outfit: flowy dress, denim jacket, and ankle booties.

Those advertising people were dangerous.

A quick powder refresh on her makeup and she was back in the living room, seated on a floor cushion across from her parents on the couch. Her mother had plated the food on the blue Noritake china and even placed a couple of flowers in a vase on the center of the coffee table. Touched by her thoughtfulness, the scent of fried chicken and rice immediately calmed her.

A quick bite wouldn't make them too late.

"Your father almost smashed your car today on the way home from the market. One big metal folding chair just sit in the middle of da street! No can judge, but whoever wen put dat chair in the middle of Main Street gotta be nutz!"

How her mother could say she wasn't one to judge, without a trace of irony, Cassandra had no idea. She laughed, "I almost did the same thing last August."

The weekend of the first high school football game, there had been a random folding chair outside of The Home Team Bar.

"Funny story about the chair. Margie, the owner of The Home Team, told me that years ago The American Legion held a pancake feed and wanted to invite everyone in town. They propped a large sign on a folding chair in the middle of Main Street where everyone driving through town would see it. Afterward, any time someone had a public event, they dragged a folding chair into the Main Street intersection and taped a big sign to it. Except one day the sign blew off. Instead, people stopped at the bar and asked Margie for the news. Nowadays people still put an empty chair in the street, and everyone knows something important is happening."

Her mother's brows knit together. "Eh, so people just drive 'round town lookin' for a bunch of cars and just join whatever party they find, huh? That's kinda funny, yah?"

"Back home, that chair wudda been smashed to pieces by all the traffic," her dad observed. "Carson is a lot different from Honolulu, for sure."

What an understatement.

"We should invited that nice boy Andy over for dinner."

"Mom, he's a thirty-something year old man. Not a boy."

"I know that, honey." Her mother patted her hand gently. "I mean, he just got one of those faces looks like a baby still."

Cassandra said, "Mom, Andy Summers and I are friends. We do fun stuff together with Murphy and his dog, Buckley. We went to obedience school together, and we're signed up for the therapy dog class starting next month. That's all it is, Mom."

Morton's Campus Security Director Andy Summers had stopped by twice while her parents were visiting to walk Murphy while Cassandra was out sightseeing with them.

"His dog Buckley paid attention good, no?" Dad observed as Murphy noisily snuffled her mother's side until she slipped him a chicken morsel.

"Buckley and Murphy had a tough year, Dad. He's much more settled now."

"Eh! If Andy train his dog that quick, he must be a natural leader," Dad continued, looking pointedly at Cassandra. "Good leader can help with the stress."

Cassandra squinted at her dad suspiciously. "Are we still talking about the dogs? Or are you trying to say something about me?"

"So what your father means is, you two got a lot of stuff the same-same. And Andy looks at you more than just a friend."

Them, too? It was bad enough her friends Meg and Cinda were constantly connecting her to Fischer, Andy, or any eligible bachelor who passed through town.

"I can't control how people look at me, Mom. Besides, I think Andy's seeing someone already. I saw them out together at The Home Team a couple of weeks ago."

"Eh, you and Fischer for real then?" Mom's eyes lit up with plenty of hope. "He got the six-pack."

Cassandra's shocked face jerked toward her mother. "Six what??"

"The six-pack. You know, when the young guys play volleyball on Ala Moana Beach they all show the six-pack."

"Mom! Since when do you check out the guys on the beaches? You're not supposed to be looking at Fischer's abs. And anyway, when would you have seen them since it's like 55 degrees here and everyone is still wearing sweaters?"

"Never said I look at any guys. But I can tell a guy's got six-pack on him, ya?"

Her father frowned slightly, as though he'd been tuned out for a few minutes then suddenly realized his wife was discussing another guy's body parts.

"Can we please focus?" Cassandra pleaded, "Enough with Fischer's abs. Let's clean up before we're late."

Her mom held her hands up in mock surrender. "Just sayin', even though he's good looking and stuff, he's kinda dark, yah?"

"What do you mean dark, Mom? He's as *haole* as a loaf of wheat bread." Her parents were like many old-school parents who never changed their beliefs about the different races and cultures, even when the whole world was trying to move on. Cassandra held her breath waiting to hear whatever misguided comment her mother was going to say about Fischer's skin tone or culture.

"Eh, I mean, he's a quiet one. Like he's thinking deep things inside while he goes about his normal day."

Oh, *that* kind of dark, phew! Cassandra was shocked by how insightful her mother was about Fischer's personality, considering they'd only met a few times.

"He fought in army combat time, Michiko." Her father said, "Memories like that change people and just become part of who they are."

Cassandra hadn't even realized her father was still listening. Dad had been stationed on a destroyer escort during the Vietnam War, although he'd been drafted toward the end and never saw combat. Still, he didn't talk much about his time in training or on the ship except to say the food wasn't great and he missed Cassandra's Mom.

It occurred to Cassandra that she'd never asked her mother what it had been like to move into her in-laws' house while her new husband was far away and unreachable on ship. For the second time in an hour, Cassandra was hit with an uncomfortable reality. She had spent many of her thirty-four years focused on her own goals and problems without paying much heed to what her parents' lives had been like at her age.

She needed to pay more attention.

"All right, enough of the heavy stuff." She waved her hands. "Let's get going!"

Walking up the lobby stairs to find their seats, Cassandra ran straight into her friend, Meg O'Brien.

"Hey there!" They did a quick shoulder bump and an awkward laugh due to Meg's basketball-sized baby bump. She was dressed in a long, black maxi dress that looked comfy yet flattering at the same time.

Cassandra felt a stab of envy as she took in Meg's healthy glow—something she was nowhere near ready to experience herself. They'd been friends since their days at Oahu State College when Meg worked as an ASL Interpreter and Cassandra was in grad school.

"I'm interpreting for the show tonight," Meg said with a cheerful smile. Her curly hair was pulled back from her face, which appeared to be wearing more makeup than usual.

"Mom is super excited about your baby shower before they fly home." Cassandra said, "I think hanging around with my parents for two weeks has spoiled Murphy."

"How so?" Meg asked.

"They've been taking him on long walks and car adventures. Normally he sleeps half the day on the little bed in the corner of my office while I work, so the activity is a big change."

Cassandra explained as she glanced at her mother, who had bounced off towards the concession stand like she was twenty years younger. Lowering her voice still further, Cassandra continued, "I'm pretty sure Mom has been slipping him leftovers when I'm not around. Last night, I noticed his breath smelled like the pineapple upside down Spam cake."

"Good to see you again, Auntie Sato!" Meg said before bending over to give her a tight hug.

"You the cutest little mama!" Her mother exclaimed and elbowed Cassandra gently, "I bet your parents excited to get one new grandbaby, yah?"

"For sure, my mom will camp out at my house just to hold the baby as much as possible."

"Bring your family back to Oahu and visit us again soon, okay?"

They got programs and her mom said, "Eh, remember those guys fighting with the swords yesterday looked scary-kine? You sure this play gonna be alright?"

Cassandra forced a smile onto her face. "They'll be extra careful, I promise." She hoped the words sounded more convincing than they felt coming out of her mouth.

Her parents went ahead of them a few paces. "Yikes," Cassandra whispered to Meg. "Yesterday in rehearsal I saw one actor jab another one's arm! I know it's just make-believe, but the blood was real."

Meg's eyes widened in surprise. "Wow, sounds intense. But I'm sure they know what they're doing, right?"

Cassandra shrugged. "I hope so."

Meg waved and headed backstage.

Finally, they reached their seats and settled in, waiting for the play to begin. Her mom's eyes drank in all the details of their great center-section seats, from the red velvet curtains that disappeared into the rafters to the ornate carvings on the box seats.

"It's so *da kine* fancy here in Nebraska!" Mom exclaimed to the stranger sitting next to her.

Cassandra sat next to her father, who gently patted his wife's hand as it rested on the armrest between them. After 39 years of marriage, they were still adorable. When they weren't bickering.

Fischer soon joined them and sat on her other side quietly reading the program. He was such a calm, contained person. He didn't need to fiddle with his phone or chat up the stranger next to him. Content to just sit and look around, he was a nice foil to the nervous chatter of her mother.

Seated in the same row, but one section to their left, Cassandra spotted Terrance Zimmerman with his wife who looked ready to walk the red carpet. Her blond hair was even longer than Cassandra's, and she wore a sparkly black dress with spaghetti straps.

To be fair, this probably was a special date night for the couple away from their kids. His glamorous wife didn't fit Cassandra's idea of the nerdy Zimmerman's perfect match. Not that she was judging.

Her parents being in town had interrupted the flow of her normal workaholic 80/20 professional schedule. Usually work took up 80% of her time. Cleaning, shopping, working out, and taking care of Murphy neatly filled the other 20%. She had always tried to avoid entangling herself in other people's relationships, but now she found her thoughts turning more and more often to love and romance. She was embarrassed to find that she was obsessing over men, wondering if she would ever get to hold her own newborn child in her arms and breathe in their soft baby scent.

Whoa! Her parents needed to leave soon.

Quickly, Cassandra snapped out of it. She wasn't looking for love on a cheap dating app! She was an academic and a career woman, with plans to move up the ranks and become president of a university someday! If they could hire a good president for Morton, that person could mentor her along the plan she'd begun years ago.

She studied Fischer's profile for a few seconds. He'd never explained his odd behavior toward Fran Morrison during the interview. How well did she really know him?

Fischer must have sensed her staring because he turned his head, flashed a smile, and gave her hand a squeeze. The lights dimmed, and the opening music interrupted her thoughts before they spiraled too far. As soon as the show started, Cassandra was completely captivated by the amazing sets and the actors' French accents —even though they were not particularly authentic. Despite her initial concerns about the dangers of swordplay and fake musket shooting, she lost herself in the drama unfolding in front of her.

Chapter Eight

CHEERS AND SHOUTS ERUPTED from the audience as two musketeers and two bandits entered the central spotlight, leaped into action, and delivered a flurry of blows at centerstage. Cassandra's heart pounded. After what she had seen of Nate and Sam's scene during rehearsal, she willed the two young men to play it cool.

The physicality of the performance was no act. Nate and Sam were sweating and grunting with each thrust and parry. Although Cassandra knew every move was rehearsed and choreographed, she couldn't help getting pulled into the action.

Suddenly Sam growled and lunged forward, his sword connecting with Nate's shoulder. Cassandra worried over whether that was part of the choreographed moves.

Nate stumbled back and seemed off balance, unable to stop the force of Sam's next attack - an overhead cut to his head that Nate took with a high parry on his guard. Nate wiped the sweat from his forehead with the sleeve of his doublet before retaliating with a blade thrust that caught Sam directly in the chest. As he struck, a loud crack echoed through the hall.

The music swelled to a crescendo and Sam stumbled back, clawing at his chest, and crashing into another group of fighters who jumped backward, startled by the unscripted movements. Nate stood frozen in the spotlight, looking at his sword with a confused expression. The musicians quieted, and a high-pitched scream erupted from the front row.

Cassandra gasped. "Is his sword ... broken?" she mumbled to Fischer.

The other actors slowed, turning toward the middle of the stage. Amid the hush, Cassandra heard an actor yell, "Sam! Sam! Are you okay?"

Shannon Bryant shoved his way into the circle of stunned actors, kneeling at Sam's side.

Cassandra stood and stepped sideways over her parents' legs out to the aisle. Deputy Scott Tate appeared alongside her in jeans and a pullover athletic top.

"What just happened?" she asked.

"That wasn't part of the story," he replied. "Call 9-1-1."

They bounded up the stairs, Cassandra's fingers trembling as she dialed.

Sam lay on the wooden stage, his chest rising and falling in quick, shallow breaths. A grimace of pain crossed his face. Blood seeped through Shannon Bryant's fingers pressed tightly to Sam's chest.

Simon Harris burst onto the left side of the stage, his eyes squinting against the bright spotlight. "House lights up!" he bellowed. "Get me a first aid kit!"

Cassandra fed the dispatch operator the Performing Arts Center address and answered her questions.

Marcus Fischer stepped forward, blocking the audience's access to the stage. Bob Soukup met him halfway up the stairs. "Is he okay? Did anyone call an ambulance? Who's in charge here?"

Harris came to stand beside Fischer, his voice laced with venom. "It sure isn't you." Spittle sprayed out of Harris's mouth while he yelled, "Back off. You've been a thorn in my butt this whole time."

Fischer neatly wedged a shoulder between them. "Let's take a breather." He clapped an arm around Harris's shoulder and push-walked him offstage away from Bob Soukup.

Andy and his date materialized from the darkness of the stage. Andy held his phone to his ear too, but then asked Cassandra, "Are you already talking to 9-1-1?"

She nodded.

"Okay, I'll get my campus security guys over here."

Harris rushed forward with the red emergency kit and dropped to his knees next to Shannon and Sam. He opened the case and handed supplies to the deputy. The two worked feverishly over Sam's prone body while the time ticked away agonizingly slow.

After a minute or two, Andy asked Tate, "How bad is it?"

Deputy Tate sighed, running his hands through his hair. "Shannon took his hand away for a few seconds and blood spurted up. It's bad."

Cassandra lowered her phone to her chest. "The dispatcher said it's going to take them over twenty minutes to get here."

She was no medical expert, but twenty minutes seemed too long for a chest wound. She took a deep breath, trying to hold in all of her emotions.

Andy proposed transporting Sam himself and meeting the ambulance on the road between Carson and the Wahoo hospital. Without hesitation, he handed his keys to the woman behind him, who, despite the chaos, remained unfazed—calm and collected, like a kindergarten teacher who had seen it all. She took the keys and headed off to pull his car around to the loading dock.

Tate looked to Cassandra. "The bleeding has slowed down. Think this is our best move?"

"I guess this is normal when you live so far from the hospital?"

Andy said, "I'll have one of our campus cruisers give us an escort. It's the fastest way to get him help."

"Let's hope so." She nodded, but inside she was scared. Losing control would do no one any good. She had to focus on helping or else things would get worse. A shudder ran up her spine at the thought of that happening.

Andy stepped around and prepared to grasp Sam's legs. He waited until Shannon made eye contact and made a lifting motion. "We're taking him. My car."

Tate stood behind Sam's shoulders and with a couple of other guys, they heaved him up and out the backstage door, leaving Cassandra alone with her thoughts. Her parents' seats were empty, and suddenly she felt like this was all her fault. Hadn't it just been yesterday when her students were teasing her about being "The Queen of Doom"? What had happened to this peaceful town since she'd arrived in August? More and more, it was feeling like Cabot Cove, Maine.

Then Fischer was at her side, his sporty scent enveloping her in its light cloud. "Let's hope that wasn't as bad as it looked," he said softly.

Tate came back, his sweatshirt slightly rumpled. "They should reach the ambulance soon," he said, giving her a reassuring glance.

Cassandra's heart still pounded, but she'd had a few minutes to replay the fight in her head. When Nate's sword broke, his forward momentum carried him into Sam's chest. It had been such a freaky accident. Maybe avoidable, but it had happened so fast.

Once again, she found herself in uncharted leadership territory. She turned slowly around and surveyed the remaining actors. Tate and Fischer approached center stage. Everyone stood in groups of two or three, either murmuring to each other or quietly staring at the blood remaining on the wooden stage.

She gently ushered the students away and turned to Tate. "We need to file an incident report, but Andy usually does that."

Tate nodded. "We don't need the whole audience to write your report. You could send them home and keep the actors and crew here until we sort it all out."

"Agreed." Grasping her hands tightly, Cassandra whispered a prayer for Sam's safety and those driving him.

Cassandra became aware of angry voices offstage. Simon Harris and Bob Soukup were arguing again. Near the first row of seats, Fran Morrison stood nicely dressed, still in her job interview outfit. She must have come as Soukup's guest to the performance. What horrible timing.

This was no way to woo a presidential candidate.

Hard to believe Cassandra had begun the day with such optimism.

"I told you weeks ago these props were too realistic," Soukup said. "No one in this audience cares if you used wooden or plastic swords. I gave money for this show to be of high quality, but where did you spend it? Not safety equipment or protective clothing, obviously. You look ridiculous up there. You botch everything you do —no wonder you're stuck in this 'podunk town' as you call it."

"You think this is my fault?" Harris said, frustration clear in his voice. "We practiced using the metal props for weeks! Shannon Bryant even checked them daily. People come here for a good show. Wooden swords just don't cut it with them. The funds you donated barely covered our basic costs, let alone special vests or shields. I'm not responsible for user error."

"You. Are. The. Director." Soukup jabbed a stubby finger at Harris with every word. "That makes you responsible for all of this! I'll have your head!"

But Harris wasn't backing down. "Look, dude," he said, gesturing towards the door. "I don't care what you do, just get lost. I've heard enough from you these last few weeks."

Cassandra's eyes flickered between the stage and the distracting bickering of Harris and Soukup. Bob Soukup, for all his lofty position in the college's hierarchy, seemed more preoccupied with how his donation had been spent on the play rather than addressing the issue at hand. Typical.

She'd let them squabble, but her priority was to ensure the safety of her students. Cassandra approached a crew member with a headset. "Can you get a few folks to usher the audience out to the lobby and make sure they don't come back inside?"

"I'll help them," Fischer volunteered.

She smiled at him. Their track record of odd dates wasn't improving tonight.

Cassandra approached the stage manager standing alone, clutching a clipboard to his chest like a lifeline. "Can I borrow that please?"

She flipped a few pages and found a blank sheet of paper. "We need your names," she announced to the nearest group of actors. "Pass it around the cast, will you? Have a seat, everyone. We need to get your contact information before you can leave."

At the sound of grumbling, Cassandra quickly added, "You can all use the bathroom and get something to eat. It's on me! Just don't leave the Arts Center." Even if she had to foot the entire bill, it was worth it to keep the peace.

Scanning the audience for her parents, she saw them exiting behind a small group of Meg O'Brien's family and Shannon's daughter. Hopefully the kids had seen nothing so graphic that they were traumatized by the fight.

But when Cassandra spotted the reporter, Derek Swanson from the *Omaha Daily News* lurking at the back of the theater, talking to the tech guy and giving her a finger wave, her heart sank.

Great. Now she'd have to make an official statement to the press. Morton College had been plagued by bad publicity for months, and this was only going to make things worse.

Simon Harris joined Cassandra and Tate near the bloody spot on the stage where Sam's body had fallen. Normally the picture of calm Indiana Jones cool, Harris's shirt was untucked, his hair sticking out like he'd been shocked. The broken tip of the metal sword lay nearby, a haunting reminder of what they'd just witnessed. Harris stared at it as though he could will it back together into one piece. He mumbled, "I've never seen one of those break before."

Nate was still leaning against the wooden balcony set piece, a broken rapier clutched in his right gloved hand.

The poor guy seemed to be in shock. Cassandra felt sorry for him. She reached out and put her hand on his shoulder. "Nate? It's Cassandra Sato," she said kindly. "Are you hurt too?"

Tears streaming through his grubby makeup, Nate lifted his face but didn't get a chance to say anything before Sheriff Hart came through the backstage door looking like he'd just stepped out of Yellowstone's central costuming, his starched brown uniform had crisp folds on the shoulders, but his pants showed the wrinkles of many hours sitting in the cruiser. He nodded at Deputy Tate and everyone standing around the edges of the stage.

Bob Soukup broke the silence by abruptly blurting out, "Finally, you're here! Now, I want to know why *this* boy," he pointed at Nate with a sausage-sized finger, "tried to kill my grandson!"

Cassandra felt her jaw drop. She hadn't known that Sam and Bob were related, but a few things made more sense now. Simon Harris appeared unfazed by the revelation, but Fischer and the deputy moved to get Soukup under control. His shouting couldn't be helping the students' anxiety levels.

The sheriff stepped closer to Nate and Cassandra.

She thanked him for coming so quickly. "Maybe you can help us figure out what happened here." She gestured toward Nate. "Let's start with him. And don't worry, I won't let the press get in the way." She shot a quick glance in Derek's direction. "No comment until we know more about Sam's condition."

Things had just gotten infinitely more complicated.

Chapter Nine

QUESTIONING THE STUDENTS REVEALED nothing that Cassandra hadn't seen with her own eyes. Despite safety protocols, several actors had gotten bruises, cuts, or twisted ankles during rehearsals and shows. Harris insisted several times that minor injuries were just a normal part of putting on a high-action play. The play had been going along fine until Nate's rapier had broken in two and Sam got injured.

Finally, Cassandra and Fischer met her parents in the theater's lobby. They were both slumped on an antique brocade couch, snoring lightly.

"They sure are cute when they're asleep," she said with a smile. "Mom finally stops talking and conks out."

It had been a long day and a stressful night.

Fischer's warm hand squeezed hers. "That wasn't exactly my idea of a romantic date night."

She raised an eyebrow, "I'm beginning to wonder if the universe is trying to tell us something."

"Maybe ... Netflix and dinner at home next time?" he teased.

She looked up into his eyes, wanting to kiss him but knowing this wasn't the time or place. So reluctantly, she let go of his hand and stepped back. "See you at work tomorrow?"

"You bet. My car's around back, so I'm going this way." Fischer smirked, "Need help getting the kids to bed?"

"Nah, brah. We're good. You go on."

She gently nudged her parents' legs, "Hey folks, we ready go home, yah?"

Her mother's eyes popped open and she hopped off the couch like she hadn't been fast asleep only seconds earlier.

"Give me a minute, and I'll pull my car around to the front door." Cassandra held up her keys and rushed toward the entrance as quickly as she could wearing her high heels.

Yet after just five steps, her mother was walking beside her. "C'mon, child. I know my old bones are plenty tired, but I can still move faster than you, yah?" She huffed along wearing her dressy black Sketchers with sequins. Her dad came too, years of marriage experience teaching him to follow at his own pace.

Outside, the drop-off driveway was deserted except for a few students from the stage crew heading off to the dorms. One woman in a long, dressy coat and heels stood alone, engrossed in her phone and tapping the screen.

Cassandra stepped closer. It was Fran Morrison. "Dr. Morrison? Fran, ... is Mr. Soukup getting his car to pick you up?"

Fran Morrison lifted her head and furrowed her brow before recognition lit up her eyes. "I met you yesterday morning, right? I'm sorry. There were so many new faces and I'm blanking on your name."

Cassandra smiled. "Cassandra Sato. No worries, I understand. Are you waiting for Mr. Soukup?"

"He went to the hospital to be with his grandson," she said as she held up her phone. "I thought I'd just call an Uber. But then I remembered there's only 200 people in this town."

"Closer to five thousand," corrected Cassandra, "but you're right, it is small. We do have an Uber driver named Clark who shuttles people to Omaha for medical appointments or to the airport. I doubt the app is going to help you tonight, though. I think his regulars just call and hire him ahead of time. Clark's not really a 'pick you up on Main Street at 10 o'clock on a Wednesday night' kind of guy."

Cassandra weighed her options: keep walking, or let Fran catch a ride with Deputy Tate, Sheriff Hart, Simon Harris, or Fischer—all of whom would probably pass nearby in a few minutes if Fran waited long enough.

At the thought of Fischer getting cozy with Fran in his sleek Audi, with its leather seats that smelled like sandalwood and outdoors,

Cassandra's selfish instincts kicked in full force. Before she knew it, her inner child blurted out, "If you don't mind squeezing in, you can ride with me and my parents."

Her parents were now waiting in the nearby faculty parking lot next to Cassandra's Honda, her mother with her arms crossed, tapping her foot and looking more than a little miffed at being stuck in the cold. Cassandra held up the key fob and beeped open the doors.

"I don't want to put you out," Fran said.

"No trouble at all." Once they were buckled in, she asked, "Where are you staying?"

"At Morton's Bed and Breakfast."

Morton College owned a bed and breakfast? That was news. Probably it made sense, since the only motel on the main highway into town was a throwback to something from the 1980s. But strange, no one had mentioned it before now.

Her mother piped up from the back seat, "Is that boy gonna be okay?"

Cassandra winced. "Sam's in good hands at the hospital now. Andy Summers is still there, and he said Sam was conscious when they took him back to the emergency room."

She wanted to gauge Fran's interest in the president's job, but talking about tonight's accident wasn't exactly a great conversation starter. "So, the interview yesterday was nice, right?" Cassandra tried to sound cheerful, despite the ever-growing dread in her chest. "Is there anything else you want to know about Morton?" Cassandra slowed the car to give them time to talk.

"I googled the college," Fran said as she looked out at the Victorian houses. "You folks have had a run of bad luck around campus lately, wouldn't you say?"

"A few unfortunate incidents," she stressed, hoping her parents wouldn't ask. She hadn't told her parents about *all* the catastrophes, knowing they worried about her enough already.

In December, she'd kept them in the loop about Interim President Winters, who was diagnosed with early onset Alzheimer's and now lived in a long-term care facility. Hence, the reason Winters' dog,

Murphy, was Cassandra's new housemate. She'd neglected to mention the other, er ...mishaps.

"More than tonight's stabbing?" Cassandra's mom leaned forward between their seats, clearly not buying it.

Cassandra gripped the steering wheel harder as she tried to stifle a laugh so uncomfortable it came out like a bark. Finally, she joked, "It's not like there's an evil overlord who's out to destroy the college or anything."

She was not the Queen of Doom.

From the back seat, a skeptical noise showed her mother's take on it.

"Come on, Mom... Tonight was an accident!"

Driving Fran Morrison was turning out to be a terrible idea.

She needed to change the subject quickly, so she asked her guest, "So what interested you about Morton College? Did you know any faculty or staff from your old jobs?"

Like Marcus Fischer, maybe? She kept her gaze forward, taking a huge gulp of air before she exhaled.

Fran chuckled, deep and sexy like a late-night radio DJ. "I've worked with plenty of people throughout my career. I couldn't tell you who I might bump into again. But I can tell you this—I like fixer-uppers. The thrill of swooping into an organization that needs work is unbeatable. Give the faculty some perks, write a killer strategic plan that makes the board of directors snap to attention, and then give donors a reason to open their wallets wide."

Her words were bold for a job candidate, but Cassandra didn't take offense. This fixer-upper wasn't her doing, and she was keen to be part of the solution.

Ten minutes later, Cassandra's phone let them know they had arrived at their destination, and she pulled up to a house on Professor's Row—the street of stately older homes with large front porches and wide sidewalks lined with mature trees. Briefly she was rendered speechless by the realization that Morton College's new bed and breakfast had a checkered history. Having once belonged to the now deceased President Gary Nielson, his widow must have sold the property to the college when she moved to Iowa.

Cassandra gawked at the charming two-story house with a warm light on the front porch and windows aglow on the upper floor. She made a mental note to look into who was maintaining the place. Guessing the Airbnb ad hadn't mentioned that guests would be sleeping in a home where someone had been murdered. Chilly pinpricks ran down her spine as she shuddered.

Fran lifted a hand and tousled her already perfect hair. "I finish what I start. After what I've seen so far, Morton College checks all the boxes. It needs a complete overhaul, down to the studs."

When Cassandra had interviewed the previous summer, she'd been blinded by the thrill of moving across the country to a new state and learning more about Midwestern culture. It wasn't until she'd been at Morton for a few months that the enormity of the changes needed had sunk in. Fran Morrison had seen right through the facade in only a couple of days.

She got out of the car and leaned her head back inside the open door. "Thanks for the ride, Cassandra. I hope, for your sake, the student is going to be okay."

As the door slammed, Cassandra gasped. *For my sake.* Plus, Fran hadn't really answered her question about if she already knew Fischer or not. Except she'd mentioned something about studs, whatever that meant.

"I like that one!" Mom announced from the back seat. "She's got spunk."

Spunk. Just what Morton College needed. Cassandra shifted into drive and pulled away from the curb.

Chapter Ten

ANDY SUMMERS WAS IN line at the Student Center's coffee shop when Cassandra and Fischer arrived after attending Fran Morrison's public presentation. Cassandra had spent most of the walk gushing about Fran's proposed options to improve enrollment strategy and maximize matriculation rates. Cassandra knew better than to put Fischer to a loyalty test, but still couldn't resist asking him, "Compared to the other applicants, Fran was more qualified by far. Do you plan to vote for her to become the new president?"

"Haven't decided." Fischer shrugged, busily tapping away on his phone app to order coffee. "Gonna wait til the third interviews are done."

The last candidate was another older white man who had made the circuit around several small private colleges in the region. On paper, he seemed as dull as dishwater.

Cassandra knew she had to make the right decision for the college more than her own relationship with Fischer. Unfortunately, her female instincts told her that having Fran Morrison in close proximity to her boyfriend Fischer might not end well.

Cassandra was skipping the meet the candidate luncheon to enjoy her parents' last full day visiting and get ready for Meg's baby shower. Fischer was also skipping the luncheon, but mostly because he disliked formal social events that were just for appearances.

Before she could leave town, she wanted a status update with Andy. "Any news?" Cassandra asked, perching on a chair between the men. The invigorating aroma of freshly brewed coffee sent Cassandra's brain instantly into turbo mode.

As usual, their physical differences were striking: Andy with his closely cropped hair and medium-weight campus security jacket. Fischer was dressed like an outdoor hiking guide, with longish dark hair and a lean, muscular frame. Andy was in decent shape, too, though his daily donut habit had taken its toll on his midsection, shaped more like a case than a six-pack.

"The sheriff and I have a meeting later this morning." Andy said, "I checked in with the hospital early this morning. Sam woke up from his surgery and talked to his mom, Rhonda. I'll let you know if I find out anything new."

Andy had nursed a crush on Cassandra when she'd first arrived in town, which had led to a few awkward moments among the three of them. But she was seeing Fischer now, and Andy had brought a date to the play last night. Good thing, too, because there wasn't room in her life for more complications right now.

"I'm glad he was able to talk to his mother."

They picked up their orders, then Cassandra brought up another worry. "I bet Shannon Bryant feels awful."

"He did a great job with the first aid," Andy said. "Totally calm and focused the whole time we drove to the hospital in Wahoo. Like he was some kind of army medic. I was impressed."

"I'm worried about Nate Parker, too," Cassandra said. "He was so quiet last night. I plan to touch base with him about seeing a counselor to talk it out. But my main question is why the sword was sharp enough to hurt Sam in the first place?"

Fischer suggested, "Maybe it wasn't sharp until it broke."

"Did either of you get a closer look before the sheriff took it?" Andy asked.

Cassandra shook her head. "No, I didn't touch it."

"It looked fairly realistic," Fischer added. "But even a blunt edge could do damage if you jab hard enough."

Cassandra said, "We probably have to shut down the play until we can provide better assurance that Morton is using safe equipment. That moment is still on replay in my head today. It was scary. We've had enough accidents on campus. And we just don't need another front-page newspaper story about our college's incompetence. I wonder whether Simon Harris or Shannon Bryant were in charge of the stage props."

Andy said, "Good question. I'll check into it for my incident report."

Fischer nodded. "I'm going to the Arts Center next and make sure the building is cleaned up from last night. I'll take a look at the stage props more closely."

"Canceling the play is going to make a lot of people angry," said Andy.

"Maybe not cancel completely, but wait until we know it's safe enough." Cassandra said, "I'll check with Dr. Gregory and see what he thinks."

"You start to wonder if there's a curse or dark force behind it all," Fischer shrugged. At first, Cassandra was taken aback by his mention of curses. Then she caught the mischievous sparkle in his clear blue eyes and the way laughter crinkled the corners. "Queen of Doom, eh?" Fischer smiled. "That's ominous."

"Not you, too."

Her father's voice broke into Cassandra's thoughts before she could make a good retort. "Marcus! Just the man I was hoping to run into. I heard there's a Spam factory nearby that gives tours. Any chance we could go tomorrow while the ladies are having their wine and cookies?"

Ever since her father had spotted the factory in their tour book, he'd been asking to go. Cassandra clenched her teeth together in a grimace. "Dad, I doubt Fischer has time... "

Fischer stood and shoved one hand in his jeans pocket, finishing off his coffee in one long swallow. "Sure. That sounds ...interesting. I'll check their hours online and get back to you."

Murphy sat at her father's feet attached to a leash. Her mother had him dressed up in a ridiculous little track jacket. She said, "We're heading over to da neighbor's house tonight to play board games. Mrs. Gill is a Scrabble expert." Mom tapped her temple with an index finger. "But no worries. I got some tricks up my sleeve, you see. Let's stop at the store on our way home. I'm going to mix a pitcher of my signature cocktails to take next door." She wiggled her eyebrows up and down knowingly.

Cassandra heard Andy snort-laugh next to her. Before Cassandra moved to Nebraska, her mother hardly ever drank anything stronger than flavored seltzer water. Now she was mixing signature cocktails?

Cassandra closed her eyes. She loved her parents, really. Yet a part of her was ready to get back to working full time and giving her complete attention to her job responsibilities. This half-time work and half-time tour guide thing was exhausting. She was much more comfortable in full work mode.

Before Andy left, he said goodbye to her parents and shook her father's hand. Once Fischer left too, Cassandra was ready to pick up her things from the office, and they could leave for the day.

"Smell that coffee," her mom said. "Can we grab one to go before we head to the Omaha zoo?"

Cassandra's dad frowned. "Today it's buying froufrou coffee. To-morrow what, huh?"

"Ah Ken, we stay on vacation, right?" Her mother patted his arm. "We deserve some treat ourselves."

Her mother grabbed the leash and headed to the ordering counter, saying, "Probably they got some biscuit for Murphy too."

"Mom, Murphy doesn't need a dog biscuit. You spoil him."

Ignoring Cassandra, her mother went on talking to the pup, "This little guy might be the only grandbaby I get here in Nebraska for a long time. Ain't that right?"

Cassandra rolled her eyes back so far in her head she thought she might see stars, but said nothing.

Cassandra noticed Sela Roberts waiting ahead of her parents at the coffee counter. Grabbing her cup, Sela quickly turned around and avoided eye contact. An international student from a Caribbean island, her mother was a government diplomat, and Sela was used to getting her way. She and Cassandra had had several run-ins, some bad, some neutral. None great.

Her mother turned to admire Sela as she sashayed around the corner wearing short shorts and an off-shoulder sweatshirt with hightop basketball shoes and a tropical printed headscarf.

"Eh, I think I need one of those head wraps," her mom said admiringly in Sela's direction. "Really makes her eyes pop!"

Picturing her mother's salt and pepper hair wrapped in a scarf like Sela's, she quickly coughed into her folded arm and forced her expression into something less incredulous.

"I think we'd better get to the car, Mom." Cassandra rasped. "After the zoo, you promised to help me finish Meg's baby quilt for her shower."

But her mother wasn't done. She turned back to the dog and loudly asked if he thought Cassandra would start a family with Fischer or the campus policeman.

If only the ground would open up and engulf her. Since that wasn't an option, Cassandra grabbed both of her parents by the arms and proclaimed: "Let's go! The animals await us!"

Chapter Eleven

G AS AND SWEETS, THE combined gas station and convenience store that shared space with the town bakery and gift shop, wasn't Cassandra's first choice for grocery shopping. But this week had been hectic, and she didn't have time to drive to a larger food market.

Clutching a bottle of cheap vodka for her mother's signature cocktail in one hand, Cassandra scanned the full whiskey shelves that were better stocked than a fancy Honolulu liquor store. She had a double mission: find something special for her dad and make a favorable impression on her neighbor Mr. Gill, because neither man would be caught dead drinking her mother's sweet, fruity concoction.

Next, Cassandra evaluated the small glass case near the gas station front counter containing the bakery's leftovers, trying to choose between a coconut cream pie or a layered, parfait-looking dessert.

Bob Soukup owned the entire building, among his many businesses, and his daughter Rhonda ran the Sweets bakery where Cassandra planned to treat her parents to fresh pastries for breakfast. Tonight the big man was running the cash register himself. She made a mental note to ask after his grandson Sam when it was her turn to pay.

People said Bob Soukup knew all the town's secrets, to the point where it often sounded like he was a small-time mob boss the way people gossiped. "Soukup knows where the bodies are buried." Cassandra mostly thought it was fanciful thinking, except she had seen his bullying first-hand when he'd yelled at his daughter Rhonda for a silly indiscretion.

Ahead, a young father juggled his toddler on one hip while he fumbled through his wallet for a credit card. The girl's fine hair was pinched together in a pencil-thin ponytail atop her head, then fell past her shoulders. Her chubby hand grabbed a long stick of beef jerky from the counter display stand, and Soukup scowled while he waited for the man to produce his payment.

The little girl was adorable, but Soukup was immune. Cassandra smiled at her over her father's shoulder and was rewarded by a wide grin that displayed tiny front teeth. Finally, the man completed his transaction, and the woman who was next in line approached the counter.

After her smiling exchange with the toddler, Cassandra pushed her cart down the next aisle, hurrying a bit, so she wouldn't be late. Her mother was thrilled at the invitation to the neighbors' house for game night. Mrs. Gill and she had chatted several times during their vacation while taking the dog for walks and weeding the flowers that grew between their houses.

Cassandra threw a few extra snacks into her cart. She sincerely hoped the Gills wouldn't mention the tree that had fallen on her house during the winter break between semesters. She'd hoped to keep that little problem a secret from her parents. They already worried enough about her moving so far from home and living alone.

As Cassandra waited for other customers to pay, she looked down the aisles to trigger her memory for anything else she needed tonight. A middle school-aged boy dressed in baggy shorts and an oversized t-shirt slowly perused the center aisle. Something about his manner—besides the fact just looking at his thin clothing made her feel cold—caught Cassandra's attention.

Just as she turned away, the boy's hand snatched a handful of something from the toiletries shelf and returned to the cavernous pocket in his shorts.

Cassandra blinked hard. Rooted to the floor, she peeked to the side to see if Soukup had been looking, but he seemed busy with the customer. She looked back at the boy who acted nonchalant. Maybe her tired eyes had played tricks on her.

Next thing she knew, he had slipped into line ahead of her, placed a small candy bar on the counter, and nodded to Soukup.

Should she say something, or had she just imagined the shoplifting?

Soukup scanned the candy bar and waited. The boy carefully pulled a couple of wadded up dollars from his other pocket. From her spot in line only a couple of feet away, Cassandra saw his feet shuffling side to side.

Soukup said, "And the other stuff too. C'mon." His thick finger stabbed a spot on the counter next to the candy bar.

The boy's shoulders twitched up. "What stuff?" He looked behind him at Cassandra, eyes wide.

"I saw you, Michael. What else do you have?"

"Nothin'! I swear."

Dark eyebrows that clashed with the thick white hair on Soukop's head, met in a deep frown so intimidating that Cassandra was tempted to empty her pockets even though she was innocent. "You got nothin' to swear on, son. What is it this time?"

Soukup waited. The overhead fluorescent light buzzed.

A big sigh came from someplace deep within the boy, and his chin met his chest in defeat. He reached into his other pocket and came out with travel-sized shampoos, body wash, toothpaste, and Tylenol.

Soukup eyed the items on the counter. "That'll be $1.25." He made change from the two dollars, placed everything in a plastic bag, and handed it over.

No way were all those items worth $1.25. Soukup was letting the boy get away with shoplifting. He hadn't charged him for everything.

"Your uncle feeling better today?"

Michael nodded but kept his eyes downcast. He snatched the bag and mumbled, "thanks," before running out of the store like his feet were on fire.

Everyone acted like Soukup was the town ogre, but he just did a huge kindness. Was his crusty persona an act? Mouth slightly open, Cassandra stared after Michael, a dry lump forming in her throat.

Her feet were frozen in place until a gruff voice interrupted her confusion. "Stand there all night and you'll sprout roots."

She jerked a little and placed the alcohol on the counter. "I'll take the layered dessert too, please."

"You keep eating my daughter's sweets, your back end is gonna be wider than a semi truck before you know it."

Nope, she had confirmation his crusty ogre persona was not an act. And she declined to mention anything nice about sending positive thoughts about his grandson. He was an odious man.

"Pivot! Pivot!"

Cassandra heard the TV through her closed bedroom door. She'd changed out of her work suit into stretchy yoga pants and an oversized University of Hawai'i hoodie perfect for a casual evening at the neighbors' house. Grabbing an elastic ponytail holder, she opened the door to find her parents laughing on the couch in the living room.

"I love this one!" Cassandra perched on the leather ottoman in front of her large leather armchair and tied her hair into a high bun. "But right after it's done, we should go next door to the Gills' house."

On screen, Chandler, Ross, and friends struggled to move Ross's large couch up a flight of stairs to his new apartment, but failing miserably.

Her father said, "I tried to convince your mother to watch a TV show made in this century, but she likes the classic stuff."

"Reminds me when all you kids stay young and living at home for real. We watched 'Friends' every week together." Her mother was breathless from laughing so hard. "New shows never get this good."

Cassandra smiled. "Correction. You wouldn't let me watch it until I was in college because you told me 'Friends' was inappropriate for someone my age. I snuck into the hallway and peeked around the corner when you thought I was in bed reading."

"I know," her father said. When Cassandra turned to him, open-mouthed, he said, "You thought you were real sneaky, but I saw you anyways. I never tell your mother."

Mom sighed in exasperation. "Why even have house rules if nobody gonna follow them?"

Dad gave Mom a pat on the back. "She turned out all right though, eh?"

Sobering, Cassandra remembered Michael, the boy at the convenience store who was obviously struggling. "I saw the weirdest thing at the store earlier." She told her parents about Bob Soukup and how he seemed like such a grouchy jerk most of the time, but let the boy keep the toiletries from his store without paying for them.

"You work with this guy sometimes, eh?"

"He's on the board of directors at the college and a major donor, so everyone is constantly tiptoeing around trying to please him. You might've seen him the other night at the play rehearsal. That was his grandson Sam who was hurt last night. Bob is such an enigma."

Her mother smiled proudly. "Bigwig or no, my daughter never sneak around somethin'."

"I've learned to be diplomatic, but also not a doormat at work. I don't even know how long I'll be in this job before I move into a better one."

Her father said, "When people do random stuff, usually mean they think something else underneath the surface. Better take some time to check out Bob Soukup's life and figure out why he acts that way."

Good advice. Cassandra would watch him more closely from now on.

"Ya know," her mother added, "I bet if you look into this Bob character, you'd find out he's a undercover superhero or something!"

Cassandra highly doubted it, but her dad didn't give her a chance to respond before shushing them. "This is the best part of this episode."

Chapter Twelve

CASSANDRA'S STOMACH GRUMBLED IN anticipation as she eyed the kolaches at the Sweets bakery, her mouth watering with every passing moment. Apparently, she wasn't the only early morning person in Carson, as the line snaked around the gift shop. The scent of cinnamon and sugar wafted over her like an intoxicating perfume as she watched Rhonda and an assistant fill orders.

"I'm a little surprised to see you here this morning," Cassandra said when it was finally her turn. Deciding between all the flavors would be tough, so she ordered two of each, eager to share them with her parents back at the house. "I heard you got to talk to Sam last night?"

"His surgery went well. They said he needs to rest," Rhonda said. "I'll go back to the hospital after the morning rush. I just hope he doesn't miss too many classes. He needs to keep his grades up."

Rhonda Soukup was mid-forties and had the wide-eyed look of someone who was always on alert for bad stuff heading their way. Cassandra never could tell if Rhonda's relationship with her father was just strained or broken, and she didn't know Rhonda well enough yet to ask such personal questions.

"What a relief Sam's feeling better. Usually professors will work with students who have medical issues. Let me know if he runs into any problems."

"I heard you lost in Scrabble last night?" Rhonda placed the kolaches in a small brown box. "I never know enough words with the letter Q."

"How'd you know?" Cassandra asked, still not used to the small town way everyone knew everyone else's business.

Rhonda smiled. "Mr. Gill comes in here every morning to buy his wife a fresh muffin, and he's a talker."

Cassandra had discovered that herself the night before. Especially after half a pitcher of Mama Sato's spiked mango guava cocktails. They'd all stayed up late on a school night talking about the cool stuff they'd seen at the Omaha Zoo, the latest town gossip, and the best tourist spots to hit during the Gills' next Hawaiian vacation. Cassandra was tired, but she only had a short time left before her parents went home.

"Mr. Gill brings her breakfast every morning! Wow, that's true love," Cassandra said.

Cassandra's father may not have bought her mother breakfast every morning, but he still started the coffeepot, and brought her a cup in bed. Every week, he cut fresh amaryllis from their yard and put them in a vase on the kitchen table—expressions of love she had taken for granted growing up.

Seeing loving couples like her parents and the Gills set the bar high. Could she check off all the boxes on her future life plan like academia, independence, financial stability, AND love, marriage, and children?

Paul had been the first man she had ever loved, and although he hadn't been part of her life for years, she couldn't let go of the dream of growing old together.

Fischer was different in almost every way compared to Paul. She hadn't realized it because of her youth, but Paul had felt like a safe harbor. They had a lot in common, their families got along, and they shared an easy companionship. If she were completely honest, Paul wanted her to stay the Waipahu girl he fell in love with.

Fischer wasn't very talkative about his feelings or his military experiences. She knew his knee injury still bothered him, but unless she specifically asked, he rarely mentioned it. She planned to think more about his behavior with Fran Morrison, but it would only be an issue if she got the president's job. Fischer's imperfections made him more complex and attractive. He walked with a confident, sexy swagger that made Cassandra want to win his trust. She wanted to know more about his childhood, his scars, his dreams. Her interest was keen enough to make her imagine children who laughed like him or snuggling up together on the couch under a soft blanket on a Saturday night.

The odds of having it all seemed impossible for Cassandra as she entered her mid-thirties in the middle of nowhere Nebraska without a serious partner. But instead of giving up hope, she resolved to take life one kolache at a time.

Cassandra wandered down the hallway of the admin building taking a lap to shake off the tightness in her legs from sitting too long, her phone to her ear. Fischer was on the other end giving her the news on *The Three Musketeers*. "Everything looks good backstage," he said. "Shannon had everything in order for the fighting equipment and props and the student stage manager is responsible to make it all ready to go."

Cassandra eyed the president's office door as she made the turn at the end of the long hallway. "Dr. Gregory is worried about liabilities and insurance coverage if we move forward with the play," Cassandra said. "We need to show support and remove roadblocks, not create more of them!"

Fischer laughed. "Gregory will think twice before canceling any shows when he sees how much backlash it could cause. I'm sure we can get a performance up and running by tomorrow night if we hear back from the lawyers soon enough. We should attend again just to make sure all goes well this time around."

Making plans together, they chatted until Cassandra reached her office suite's wing of the hallway and ended the call.

Back at her desk, Cassandra noticed an incoming email from Derek Swanson, the reporter she knew from the *Omaha Daily News*. He was asking for an update about the injured student and the timeline of the play. Cassandra groaned. She wasn't a spokesperson for the college, so why was he even asking her? With a sigh, she quickly deleted his message and tried to forget about it. Still, the heavy feeling of accountability sat on her head like a crown, and she prayed that doom wasn't right around the corner.

Before Cassandra could think any further on the matter, she heard a knock on her open door and saw Andy Summers standing there with a bag from the Runza drive thru. "What's up?" he asked.

The yeasty smell of fresh bread and greasy onion rings made her stomach growl even though she'd eaten not one, but two kolaches earlier.

Cassandra reached for her warm coffee cup and glanced at her watch—11:32 in the morning. "That depends. Are you here to feed me or for intel?"

Andy blushed all the way to the blond hairs of his buzz cut, smiling. "Can't it be both?"

Cassandra couldn't stifle her own smile back at him, grateful for their intermittent food breaks. She took a bite of an onion ring and moaned a little while the gloomy doom shrunk into a pinhole.

"Just wanted to update you on that meeting with the sheriff," he began between bites of fries. "Nate's broken sword has some suspicious marks on it. Looks like they were made by a tool."

"What do you mean, made by a tool? Someone wanted the sword to break?"

Andy shrugged. "Not sure yet, but it's a possibility. Sheriff is still investigating."

Cassandra sat back in her chair, a weight settling on her shoulders. How in the world did an accidental campus injury on private property turn into a potential criminal investigation? "We were there. It was a freak accident."

"Well, it wasn't too long back that we had a couple of so-called freak accidents that turned out to be intentional. Someone complained to the sheriff that Morton didn't do enough to sidestep this mess."

The bloody stain on the stage floor flashed in Cassandra's mind. The onion ring came halfway up her esophagus in a gag reflex. She let out a big sigh, and pressed her fingers against her temple.

After a few more minutes of casual weather talk, Andy gathered the trash from his side of the desk. "We saved Sam Soukup's life, no doubt about it. The truth will come out when everything gets sorted." Andy gave her a reassuring smile. "Everything's gonna work out, don't worry. We're good."

In the months Cassandra had worked at Morton College, each time the sheriff's office got involved, "we're good" had not been her first thought.

Chapter Thirteen

B EFORE SHE HAD TIME to respond, two quick raps on her closed office door prompted Andy to clear out of his seat. "I gotta go anyway."

Andy opened the door. Devon stood to the side and let him pass. "Nate's here."

Andy glanced over his shoulder at her and raised his eyebrows in a silent question. She gave him a microscopic shrug while Devon and Nate took seats in the chairs facing Cassandra's desk.

Nate's wavy hair came to his eyebrows and covered his ears. His slightly round face featured light brown freckles sprinkled across his nose. Guarded eyes stared at an imaginary point in the middle of her desktop.

When she asked how he was feeling, he mumbled, "Fine."

"Thanks for coming in," Cassandra said. "Are you doing okay since the other night?"

Devon and Nate looked at each other and shook their heads. Uncomfortably.

She tried an easier question. "What made you and Sam join the play? Are either of you theater majors?"

Devon laughed, and Nate cracked a smile. "Swords," they said in unison.

"I'm a business major. Sam and I are in Dr. Harris's anthropology class," Nate said. "Harris kept yammering about how he needed more guys to try out for the play. Extra credit, he promised. I failed my first test, so I needed all the points." Nate paused while the corners of his eyes glistened with tears. "Sam said it'd be fun."

She was surprised they were good enough actors without previous experience. Usually kids earning extra credit just helped build the sets or ran the lighting equipment.

"Sam said the only thing girls like more than a guy in uniform, is a guy in uniform with a big sword."

Devon rolled his eyes. "Two months I've listened to these yahoos and their big sword jokes."

Nate elbowed him. "You could have tried out, too." He had perked up a little. Clearly, he and Devon were good friends.

Devon laughed. "Nah, it's been enough fun keeping you two from killing each other."

There was an awkward pause while all three of them went silent as those words sunk in.

Devon's face turned red. "I didn't mean--"

"I know what you meant," Nate said. "I couldn't stop it. The sword broke."

"I attended the play," said Cassandra. "It happened so suddenly. Did you not have any warning that the blade was weak?"

His gaze dropped back to the desktop. "I dunno." He shrugged. "We were just doing our scene like we rehearsed a bunch of times."

Devon lowered his chin and raised one eyebrow at Nate.

"Dude." Nate's eyes widened innocently, and he shook his head. "I told you it was nothing."

"I told you to come talk to Dr. Sato before the play. Kids are saying you hurt him on purpose."

Cassandra watched quietly as they tossed the proverbial hot potato back and forth.

"It was an accident," Nate said, his cheeks flushing.

"I'm just telling you what people are saying," said Devon.

"I call a time-out," Cassandra muttered as she threw up her hands in frustration. They sounded like two nine-year-olds bickering.

Devon leaned forward and said more emphatically, "Nate doesn't understand because he has two parents and he can actually afford it. You could have bought your own game system."

"I have a job you know, bro." Nate snapped back, "I work hard for my money instead of cashing scholarship and financial aid checks and using them for camping equipment and who knows what."

Game system? What about the play? And scholarship checks? That was news to Cassandra. "We aren't talking about the play anymore, are we?" So often her job felt like being a sports referee.

"I wasn't actually stealing it, you idiot," Nate said. "I just wanted to get Sam's attention. He talked about taking a backpacking trip around Europe. But he has to pay his fair share. I always meant to give it back when Sam got caught up on the bills. You and I shouldn't have to pay his bills, too. It's not fair."

When she heard the word steal, Cassandra stood up and put her hands on the desk. "One of you better come clean. Now."

Devon said, "Those two have been passive aggressive fighting for months. Sam owed us money for utilities and TV. If he takes off adventuring for the summer, we have rent due in a week, and Sam still owes us from last month."

Cassandra looked at Nate, "Did you take Sam's stuff?"

He shot Devon an exasperated look. Devon's head nodded towards Cassandra. "Just tell her. You only did it to piss off Sam."

Nate closed his eyes. "I took his game system and gave it to my girlfriend for safe-keeping until he pays his bills. Then I'm going to give it back."

Ah. Roommate problems. Cassandra knew their story still had huge gaps, but she had plenty of experience dealing with this issue. Cassandra crossed her arms over her chest. "That's not how it works."

Technically this was a disciplinary code infraction, but Cassandra believed in second chances. Since they came to her before Sam complained, she decided to give Nate time to make it right. "Look, I won't write you up if you return the game system to Sam immediately."

Nate blew out a sigh. "Well, you see. I would give it back, if I had it. But I don't. Have it. Anymore."

"Because..." Cassandra let her stink eye glare do the talking.

"The thing is," he spoke at the floor. "I broke up with my girlfriend and I haven't talked to her for a few days."

Cassandra sighed. With each passing moment, Nate seemed less like the sweet dog lover she'd first met. "Oh, for crying out loud! Get your roommate's Xbox back. I want it returned to his room before Sam gets out of the hospital."

"But—"

"This has gone on long enough." Cassandra said sternly. "Your friend is hurt in the hospital. Don't make the situation worse than it should be."

Nate slumped forward in his chair, his righteous anger seeping out of him. Devon recognized the cue to leave and stood, nudging his buddy's arm. "I'll go with you to ask her. How bad can it be?"

After they left, Cassandra refilled her coffee mug and looked outside the large window facing into the quad. The edges of the grass had turned green, and buds formed on the surrounding trees.

She thought back to Andy Summers' earlier assurance that the college was good as far as liability was concerned. The night of the play they had responded quickly to Sam's injury and gotten him immediate medical care.

But if the previous arguments between Nate and Sam became part of the sheriff's official investigation, Nate could be in a lot more trouble than getting written up for relocating his roommate's game system.

Cassandra was deep into her email inbox when her phone buzzed.

Rachel Nagle

The sheriff just took Dr. Bryant for questioning!! Dr. Harris is very upset!! Please help us at the Arts Center ASAP.

As she quickstepped across campus to the theater building, Cassandra allowed a prideful glimmer to warm her chest. People on campus appreciated her presence in stressful situations and that felt good. Unfortunately, there were far too many stressful situations around here.

When Cassandra arrived backstage, she was met with an overwhelming smell of old costumes, musty equipment, and the pungent odor of harsh chemicals that had been used to clean up the spilled blood.

Rachel hadn't exaggerated the situation. Sheriff Hart and Shannon Bryant were probably already at the sheriff's office on Main Street, and an uproar had taken their place.

Around twenty students crowded on stage with piles of equipment and costumes heaped in front of them. She approached from the side between the curtains where she had watched the rehearsal. Andy Summers and two campus police officers were on the other side, examining the rigging for the curtains and lights. Simon Harris came up to her carrying a clipboard and bellowed, "How are we expected to work under these conditions?" A speck of white spittle had lodged in the corner of his mouth. "The show must go on!"

Cassandra raised an eyebrow. "Are you holding your class here? In the *theater.*"

Recognizing her student workers, Rachel and Lance, Cassandra approached them. "What's going on?"

Rachel whispered, "Sam Soukup is one of our Death 101 classmates, so some of us volunteered to help Dr. Harris."

"Wow, that's really nice of you to help Sam and Nate."

Lance, one of the Deaf students on campus, wrinkled his nose and signed in ASL, *We're getting extra credit points for being here. I know those guys some.* He held his hand out and rocked it in a so-so gesture. *Nate can be a hothead, and Sam is kinda intense.*

Rachel nodded and signed while she spoke. "I hope Sam gets better soon. He's planning to backpack across Spain this summer. How cool is that?"

Cassandra said, "That sounds good, but did you say Dr. Bryant was arrested?"

Lance shrugged, but Rachel clarified, "I heard them say questioning. Is that different than being arrested?"

"Let's hope so," said Cassandra.

"We gathered all the costumes and equipment from the other night so the police can inspect them." Rachel gestured to the stuff on stage. "We heard they found something wrong with Nate's sword."

Andy had mentioned suspicious marks on Nate's sword. Cassandra shook her head, baffled at how quickly word had spread. "What about Dr. Bryant?"

Lance signed, *While we were checking out the props, the sheriff found a set of filing tools in Dr. Bryant's equipment bag.*

Rachel said, "The police think maybe Nate's sword was weakened before the fight."

"That's a big leap, Rachel," said Cassandra. "Maybe it just hit wrong while they were fencing. I'm sure props could break with enough force."

But Rachel shook her head. "One file in the set was missing!" Rachel hissed, "What if someone purposefully broke Nate's blade?"

It made sense for the combat coach to have stage equipment and tools. But who would ever suspect Shannon Bryant of wanting to sabotage the play by breaking the props?

Lance added, *Anyone on the set had access to the tool bag. Suspicious though, huh?*

"There has to be a logical explanation," said Cassandra.

Andy Summers approached the circle of students and gear onstage. "Dr. Harris, I thought your Death 101 class discussed the *medical* aspects of dying, not role playing *CSI* episodes?"

"We practiced *The Three Musketeers* for weeks, and several nights are sold out," Harris replied indignantly. "Your department moves like a herd of sloths. My students kindly offered to help get us back on track."

Andy waved off the students, "Y'all can leave it to us now."

He was smiling as the students filed down the aisle and out the doors, but Cassandra could tell he was seconds away from having Simon Harris ushered out as well. He locked eyes with Cassandra. "You too. Morton's campus security doesn't need help from students ...or administration."

Cassandra stood with arms crossed, an unspoken challenge in her eyes. "What gives?"

Andy raked a hand through his hair and answered as diplomatically as he could. "The students already went through a lot of the gear and clothing. Who knows what clues they've messed up."

Cassandra gave him stink eye back.

She counted her fingers one by one, emphasizing each point. "Let's not forget who risked their life to figure out what was happening in the biology lab? Who realized what was wrong with Dr. Winters? And who helped resolve the whole Chinese espionage thing? Maybe I should apply for *your* job instead of trying for president."

"Ouch." Summers placed a hand across his heart dramatically. "That is just hurtful, and you know it."

"Stop underestimating me," Cassandra warned.

"Duly noted." Summers sauntered away without another word.

So much for being the mature, calm voice of reason. This place was getting to her.

Chapter Fourteen

C ASSANDRA CRAMMED INTO HER tiny kitchen with Cinda Weller, Gia Torres, and her mom, putting the finishing touches on the food before Meg arrived for her baby shower. Although Cassandra and Meg went way back to their Oahu State College days together, Cinda and Gia were newer friends. Cinda was Director of Counseling and Career Services, and Gia, a Poli Sci professor. It felt good to be settling into new friendships finally.

It was time for a pre-game pep talk.

"Look, this is Meg's special moment. Let's try to keep the focus on her and our excitement about the baby. I know people will talk about *The Three Musketeers* and Sam's condition. Together, we can shift the conversation away from the gossip and drama to more pleasant topics. Deal?"

"You betcha," Cinda patted her shoulder. "I'm a trained therapist. I'm an expert distracter."

She plucked a chunk of Cassandra's mom's home made mango bread from a serving tray and popped it into her mouth. "Wow, this is so fresh and flavorful," Cinda said as she swallowed the bite. "It tastes like you just picked them off the mango tree."

Just then, Meg arrived and hugged each of them hello.

With five women, the kitchen was now over capacity. Cassandra paused while gratitude for her new life hit her hard, taking away her breath for a moment. She still held the second loaf of mango bread her mother had wrapped in aluminum foil and carried on the plane to Nebraska. Having good friends and her mother under her own roof was the fulfillment of one aspect of her dream. Her eyes welled up, and

she wondered where the emotions came from. With quick counting, she realized it was most likely from monthly hormones.

Cassandra squeezed past Meg's tummy to reach the serving tray
on the small gate-leg table.

Her mother said, "Glad you like the mango bread, eh Cinda. It's
my mother's secret recipe. Almost ended up in the trash bin."

Cinda exclaimed, "That would be a crime, ma'am."

"The real criminal was that handsy TSA agent at the Honolulu
airport who insisted on inspecting my frozen breads!" Her mom
grimaced. "A big lug with grimy hands, that one!"

Cassandra had heard the story several times already, so she
focused on removing the plastic wrap layer under the aluminum
foil and carefully slicing the loaf.

Mom said, "First, he touched people's *suitcases*, then patted
down their *clothes*. Then, he thinks he goin' check my *food*! He
opened the foil and started to open the plastic wrap!"

Gia gasped, "No rubber gloves?"

Cassandra picked up the story, "Daddy said that Mama pinned
that poor TSA guy with a stink eye so powerful that sweat broke
out on his forehead! He leaned over to the lady agent next to him
and pointed to the breads. 'I'm supposed to open these and make
sure they're just baked goods, right?'"

"He probably planned to sneak my breads to the break room and
eat them later when no one was looking," Mom scoffed.

Cassandra said, "The TSA lady looked Mama up and down and
said, 'It's bread, Frank. Let it go.'"

Mom nodded once, decisively. Woe to any man who crossed
Mama Sato.

Later, they sat in Cassandra's living room while Meg opened a
small pile of gifts stacked on the coffee table.

"You look so cute, Meg!" Cassandra's neighbor Mrs. Gill gushed,
"Like you're hiding a basketball under your dress."

Meg's skin glowed with happiness and good health. She wore
a thigh-length Bohemian patterned dress over coordinating gray
leggings.

"I bet you're having lots of wild sex too, right?" Cinda fanned her face with exaggerated movements. "Geez, I remember those red-hot hormones before I had my second son. They could have melted an iceberg!" She raised what was left of her mimosa in a silent salute and gave the ladies a roguish wink. "After the birth, I felt like a giant dairy cow and barely slept three hours a night. Had to keep Jacob away from me for three whole months!"

Meg and Gia gaped at Cinda with wide eyes. Cassandra felt her cheeks heat up like a furnace. She wasn't exactly a prude, but yikes. She did not want pre-birth sex scenes between Jacob and Cinda Weller playing in her head.

Cinda simply winked and said, "Oh come on now, y'all! It ain't no secret! You already got your little boy Meg, you know how it all works. Anyway, you look fabulous, honey!"

"It's these yoga pants." Meg grasped fistfuls of her gray waistband and yanked them away from her belly bump. "Supportive, and stretchy. I'm never wearing jeans again."

Cassandra laughed. "Remember when those yoga pants first became popular on campus? You and I swore we'd never wear them out of the house unless we were going to a workout?"

"I take back every snarky thing I ever said about yoga pants. They're even better than sliced mango bread," Meg vowed.

Cassandra nodded. She still wasn't comfortable wearing a skimpy sports bra and yoga pants to the grocery store without a jacket or something over top. But for house cleaning and hanging out at home, she mostly lived in them.

Meg opened Cassandra's gift: a pink, baby-sized Hawaiian quilt with a geisha girl motif appliquéd on top.

"I don't know how you found time to make this, but it's beautiful." Meg said, "You're so talented!"

"You sew?" Cinda exclaimed.

Meg had already opened an intricately crocheted baby blanket from Cinda, who said, "All I sew for the boys is Batman pajamas."

"Midwestern farm wives aren't the only crafty people, you know," said Cassandra. "Japanese women have sewn stuff for millennia. And have you never seen Hawaiian quilts?"

"I just remember hearing about your surfing days. I thought you were a studious jock." Cinda balled up the wrapping paper and stuffed it into the trash bag. "I'm okay with your softer side."

Cassandra's watch beeped and displayed Deputy Tate's phone number. She groaned to herself. It had been a long day, and bad news was the last thing she wanted to hear.

Moving quickly into her bedroom, Cassandra closed the door and answered the call.

"Cassandra?" His voice was all business. Her heart fluttered in anticipation of more bad news.

"Sam Soukup woke up, and I went to the hospital to take his statement. He mentioned a missing video game console?"

Ugh. Looked like all the roommate dirty laundry was coming out. She admitted, "I am aware. But I believe they were working on getting it back to Sam."

He said, "So there's more to it between these two. Sam seemed to think his roommates were out to get him. Pretty big chip on his shoulder, if you ask me."

She had seen all kinds of roommate squabbles before, and these fell into the normal range in her estimation.

"I'll need to bring Nate in for questioning tomorrow."

"Thanks for the communication," she said. "I'll talk with Simon Harris, the play director, tomorrow. Does this mean you're going to free Shannon Bryant?"

"We already did," Deputy Tate said before adding with a hint of concern in his voice, "Your mom and dad haven't given us their accounts of what occurred at the show yet. Sheriff Hart is breathing down my neck to hear from them. I understand they attended a rehearsal with you and witnessed the first time Sam and Nate crossed swords, so to speak."

Cassandra laughed uneasily at the thought of her parents observing anything but each other during the rehearsal. "My mom and dad were probably too busy playing with my dog to pay attention."

"Sheriff Hart is on me to get their statements. Maybe they saw someone acting strangely around the props."

Cassandra sighed loudly as she imagined her parents being questioned by Sheriff Hart during their Nebraska vacation. "Look, I've been with my mother practically every second these past two weeks," she said in a weary voice, "and I can guarantee that she knows nothing about any fencing accidents." Her voice rose in pitch. "I love them very much, but it's time for them to go home. Trust me, Nebraska is more peaceful without Mama Sato and my dad."

She hung up and went to the bathroom to wash her hands with cool water. The ominous dread she'd been feeling all week whispered, *I told you it would get worse.*

When she returned to the living room, they were finishing a game of guess how many diapers made up the diaper cake.

"That was Deputy Tate on the phone." Cassandra's hand shook a little. "The good news is they sent Shannon Bryant home."

"So did they find the missing tool from his bag?" Meg asked. "It seems obvious the broken sword was an accident ...What's the bad news?"

"Sam woke up and told Tate about some roommate drama between him and Nate. The deputy will pick Nate up tomorrow for questioning."

"Let me get this straight," Meg said. "They think Nate tried to hurt Sam intentionally? If he was mad at him, why wouldn't he just short sheet his bed, or throw a punch like a normal roommate?"

Gia said, "Another arrest won't help our presidential search process at all. Our third candidate interviews are in a few days. What kind of impression is all of this going to make?"

"If we can scare off that John Goodman dude, I'm all for it." Cassandra's eyes widened, and she pressed her fingers to her lips. "Oops. Did I say that out loud?"

"Don't worry, your snarky side is safe with us," Cinda assured her. "You're obviously tired of playing nice with Interim President Gregory and the search committee politics. The feisty VP we know and love doesn't wait for good things to happen. You should be running this place by now."

"I need more experience before I can apply for the job. But all the experience I've gotten so far is putting out these never-ending fires."

"You see these gray hairs?" Gia sat taller, her pretty cardigan, large gold earrings, and necklace perfectly matched. Gia always looked like she was ready for a fashion show. "In my *lengthy* experience, I've seen leadership changes at all levels. You young folk can talk about manifesting success and envisioning your perfect world, but putting out fires takes precedence on any job from VP," Gia threw a pointed glance at Cassandra, then Meg, "to Mommy."

Cinda turned to Cassandra, asking, "Can you count on Fischer to vote the same as you and Gia after the next interview?"

"I thought we agreed on the best kind of temperament for Morton's next president. But sometimes I feel like we just don't see the world the same way. I used to think it was because he held things back from me. Maybe that was just an excuse."

"Lately this school has been a bigger mess than a hound dog in a henhouse. We've got to turn it around soon," Cinda said.

Another catastrophe in the making on her watch. Without saying it in so many words, Cinda seemed to imply things had been better at Morton before Cassandra came along. Cassandra felt the tears pooling in her eyes, to her embarrassment. "Maybe the students were right," she finally said in a quiet voice. "Maybe it's not a coincidence. Maybe I am the Queen of Doom!"

Cinda leaned over to Cassandra, "That's a bit much for one person to fix."

The women laughed. "Oh dear!" Gia said. "Don't be discouraged as long as you're doing your best."

Cassandra lurched off the couch and rushed into the kitchen, wiping away the stupid tears. Behind her, she heard Meg announce, "Mama Sato, did I spy your homemade pineapple upside-down Spam cake in the kitchen? Who else wants a piece?"

Cassandra quietly took the steps to the basement and grabbed a basket of clean laundry.

Several minutes later, Meg appeared by her side, grabbed a bedsheet, and folded it up. "I thought I had dibs on the hormonal mood swings this week," she said with a mischievous grin. "Wait, you aren't pregnant too, are you?"

Meg had an uncanny knack for saying the most outrageous things. The absurdity of the question made Cassandra giggle. "Folding laundry soothes me. You take a crumply towel, fold it into neat thirds, and smooth the wrinkles out. Why can't life be so simple?"

Meg chuckled softly, "Because you're a more complex organism than a bath towel?"

Cassandra smiled a little. "I guess I am."

"Look," Meg said, "we've all been through a lot, but you're doing an incredible job handling it all. Everyone looks to you for answers, and you're doing the best you can. That should be enough."

The words of encouragement and support felt like a balm to Cassandra's soul. She took a deep breath and wiped away the last of her tears. "Thank you, Meg."

So much for avoiding gossip and drama. It was time to take her own advice. She had to find a way to handle this situation with grace and integrity. This was her chance to make it right. Not just for Nate, Sam, and the college, but for herself, too.

The baby shower was soon over, and Meg waddled out the front door in front of them to her car in the driveway.

Meg embraced Cassandra's mom with a tight squeeze. "I'm going to miss you, Auntie Michiko. I wish you'd still be here when our little babe makes her grand entrance."

"Just wait a while and then your family can come visit us in Hawai'i." Mom said, "You always have a place at our house."

Cassandra picked up a box filled with gifts and bags and filled Meg's trunk with her loot. "Aw, sweetie. My mom sure does love you."

Meg wiped both her cheeks. "See? Plenty of hormonal mood swings to go around."

Fischer's Audi glided to the curb, and Cassandra's dad emerged from the passenger seat with a smile like an eight-year-old who just went to the circus. He clutched a Runza takeout bag, and the scent of Spam and onion rings hung in the air around him.

"How was your tour of the Spam factory, dear?" Mom asked.

"It was good," Dad said, still beaming. "They were really nice to us when they found out we were from Hawai'i. Our tour guide joked that

Hawaii residents eat more Spam than a Monty Python movie each year. Oh ho, he was funny. The gift shop was kinda small though."

Fischer opened the trunk and pulled out a paper bag full of something heavy. He handed it to Cassandra.

"Dad, you can buy Spam at home, right?" she said, looking in the bag. "What's all this?"

"I replenished your supply and got some extra for your friends," he said, winking.

Cassandra smothered a grin, imagining how her Nebraska friends were going to react to the unusual flavors like Italian Spam or Teriyaki Spam.

The house had been quiet for maybe fifteen minutes and Cassandra was wiping the kitchen sink clean when she got a text from Andy. He had gotten clearance from the sheriff to talk to Sam Soukup at the hospital.

Andy Summers

> Do you want to be there when I talk to him?

Every roommate dispute had two sides. Or in this case, three. Talking to Sam might give her a clearer picture of how to resolve the situation.

Cassandra

> Absolutely! But I'm gonna be late to work tomorrow 'cause I gotta bring my parents to the airport first. Earliest I can be there is noon.

Andy Summers

> *It's a date.*

Cassandra finished cleaning up, and decided to call it a night.

Chapter Fifteen

ONCE CASSANDRA DROPPED HER parents off at the Omaha airport, she floored it back to town, enjoying the peace—until Murphy, vibrating with excitement in the back seat, decided to express his enthusiasm in the most dramatic way possible.

One gut-churning retch later, her leather upholstery was covered in what she could only describe as "canine abstract art."

By the time she scrubbed the car, showered, and changed, she barely had enough energy left to meet Andy—let alone pretend like she hadn't just survived a biological warfare incident in her own vehicle.

Cassandra swung into the Gas and Sweets parking lot, her tires screeching against the curb like a scene from an action movie. She needed a pastry. Immediately. Possibly two, if she was going to emotionally recover from Murphy's backseat betrayal and focus on Sam.

Instead of Rhonda, a college aged boy with Justin Bieber hair and wire-framed glasses was working the counter. She didn't know which kind of pastry was Sam's favorite, so she got three flavors and hoped one of them was right. Just in case, Cassandra also grabbed a couple extras for her and Andy to eat on the drive over.

A few minutes later, she made her way to the staff parking lot, where Andy was already waiting in his college cruiser.

"You're late," Andy barked.

Cassandra waved the bakery bag. "But I've got kolaches."

Andy's eyes lit up, and he grabbed one before taking a huge bite, apple filling spilling down his chin. "All is forgiven," he said with a full mouth.

On the way to the hospital, she prayed that the sugar rush would make Sam more amenable to dealing with Nate. Roommate squabbles shouldn't lead to criminal charges if handled judiciously.

Cassandra had been to Wahoo Hospital too many times during her short tenure at Morton College. She knew the hallways well enough to navigate on autopilot, which was both convenient and deeply unsettling.

The air smelled the same as every hospital Cassandra had ever visited, with its curious mix of disinfectant, urine, and sadness. It caught in her throat, triggering a flash of grief for Paul, her fiancé, whose battle with illness had ended in a place just like this. She swallowed hard, willing the memory back into its box. At least now, she had a few hopeful images to counterbalance the weight of loss—patients who had walked out of here stronger.

She and Andy ambled down the hall, peeking into rooms as they passed, glimpsing patients in various stages of recovery. The usual hospital hum surrounded them: murmured conversations, the distant beep of monitors, the rhythmic squeak of a cart's wheels.

But when they reached Sam's room, an eerie stillness settled over them. The blinds were drawn tight. The only sound was their footsteps on the tile and a staff member smoothing out the bed linens.

Cassandra and Andy locked eyes, unease creeping in. They spoke over each other.

"Did they move Sam to a different floor?"

"Was he discharged?"

The woman turned, and in an instant, Cassandra knew. Her face collapsed like a shade being pulled down.

"I'm so sorry."

Ice water flooded Cassandra's veins. No. Not again. Not Sam.

Barely containing their alarm, they rushed to the nurse's station, their words tumbling over each other. When they identified themselves as Morton College staff, the head nurse paled. Her voice softened, but there was no cushioning the blow.

"Sam passed away an hour ago. A blood clot. Nothing we could do."

They were too late.

The words echoed in Cassandra's head, hollow and final. *Too late.*

Cassandra felt her insides tighten and her throat close up as the tears swelled behind her eyes, her grip on the bakery bag pressing down with all her strength to keep her hands from shaking. On wobbly legs they walked into the nearest waiting room and sank into armchairs. Her breaths came in short gasps. She closed her eyes and called on her many years of yoga practice to slow and control her breathing.

When she peeked to the side, she noticed Andy bent forward, elbows on his knees, while he wiped tears from his squinted eyes. She patted his back and looked around the waiting room. In a corner, Rhonda Soukup slouched on a sofa, legs folded up to her chest, staring unseeingly into space while an older woman wearing a volunteer's lab coat rubbed her upper arm.

Nudging Andy with her knee, Cassandra lifted her chin to get him to look at Rhonda. When Andy saw her, he shook his head in confusion. Cassandra nodded to him and mouthed, *Sam's mom.*

Again he shook his head, but she was already standing up. She walked over and crouched to Rhonda's level. Cassandra said, "Rhonda? We just heard. I'm sorry about Sam."

At first, Rhonda's unfocused gaze tracked her voice, but after a couple of seconds she recognized Cassandra and nodded. She unfolded her legs and leaned forward for a hug.

"I'm so very sorry," Cassandra repeated soothingly while patting her back. Rhonda hung on for longer than Cassandra was comfortable with. But having been on the other end of the hugs before, she knew to wait until Rhonda was ready to let go.

"I talked to him for a bit last night before he fell asleep," Rhonda's puffy eyes stared at her hands. "He wanted to know why none of his friends had visited him yet. I told him I'd heard from the play director, and a professor, and that everyone sent him good wishes."

Cassandra rested a reassuring hand on Rhonda's arm. "We've all been thinking of Sam. I talked to his roommates earlier this afternoon."

"I remember he said, 'maybe now I'll get my Xbox back.'" Rhonda sniffled, "Not sure what he meant, but you know kids. I wanted him to live at home with me to save money, but no. He had to live on campus with his buddies."

To save money? Her father, Bob Soukup, was one of the richest men in town, the owner of several businesses and community initiatives.

Cassandra's confusion must have shown on her face, because Rhonda added, "There's a long story behind it all, but we don't accept money from my family. I moved away when Sam was little so my father wouldn't infect him with his greedy power grabbing. We moved back to Carson a couple of years ago after my ex and I split up."

Remembering a couple of the father/daughter skirmishes Cassandra had witnessed, she wasn't surprised that even Bob Soukup's own daughter didn't seem to like him. Sad that he had amassed money and power but couldn't buy his family's goodwill.

Cassandra said, "Well I understand it's complex, but learning to live with roommates is a good lesson for most kids."

Just thinking of how Devon and Nate would react to the news of Sam's death made Cassandra shudder with dread.

Rhonda said, "I don't think Sam was getting along with them lately. He'd mentioned wanting to move out of their apartment after the semester. He doesn't--he *didn't*," she corrected herself, "tell me details about his feelings, but I know something's been up. Even though my father can be a grump, he has a soft spot for Sam. He's been keeping a closer eye on him, and I worry he's been giving Sam bad advice."

Cassandra briefly considered sharing the news about Shannon Bryant being questioned by the police, but decided now wasn't the time. "I'm glad you were able to talk to Sam last night, and I wish I could say something to make you feel better."

She knew from experience that most likely Rhonda wouldn't remember any of their conversation. Cassandra steeled herself, gave Rhonda's hand a brief squeeze, and stepped aside to stand with Andy. "We'll touch base with you when you want to talk more." But Cassandra couldn't get the words out without her throat catching with emotion again.

Cassandra felt Andy's presence behind her as they walked out of the hospital in silence. When they finally reached the parking lot, she couldn't keep up the facade any longer and crumpled into tears in his arms, overwhelmed by everything that had happened. So many questions still unanswered. It seemed impossible to piece together the story of what had taken Sam away from his mother so soon.

Once back in the car, Cassandra dug in her bag for a tissue, blew her nose, and cleaned up her face using the visor mirror. The waterproof makeup around her eyes had done its job and except for a little extra redness she was good to go back to work. However, her psyche needed more than a quick fix.

She hadn't even realized she carried the brown paper bakery bag back to the car, but there it was on the center console. "I was so ready to walk into the room, give Sam some treats, and cheer him up for a while before he was released." She neatly refolded the top where she had crumpled it into a ball earlier.

Andy nodded, watching her carefully like he feared she would erupt into tears again. "Me too. I just had a few questions to finish up my incident report."

"This is going to change the sheriff's investigation isn't it?"

"It might have been an accident," Andy said. "But the sheriff has to check into the markings on Nate's sword. If it was tampered with..." he shrugged and let his words trail off.

"We know all three roommates have been feuding for months." Cassandra added. "When I saw Nate and Sam's sword fight during the dress rehearsal, it looked awfully authentic to me."

She just couldn't buy into the idea that Nate made an elaborate plan to break his sword and stab Sam.

Nothing made sense.

Andy said, "The sheriff will question Nate, but without any hard evidence, it's tough to prove Nate deliberately plotted it all out ahead of time. It's more likely he just let his emotions spill over into the scene."

When they pulled up to the college, Cassandra saw a county sheriff's cruiser blocking their parking spot. Deputy Tate stepped out from the back door of the admin building carrying a bag, and she felt her stomach lurch.

"We tracked down what we presume is the metal file used to weaken Nate's sword," Tate reported.

That could be the break-through they needed. Now maybe they'd have proof it was an accident after all.

Tate revealed a blue backpack. "This belongs to Nate Parker," he said gruffly. "We'll run tests to check for prints, but it doesn't look good."

Cassandra felt like someone had punched her. She had wanted to believe it was all an accident, but the evidence was pointing to something more sinister. She wished for some way to undo what had happened, but it was too late for that. She was determined to get justice and answers no matter what it took.

As Andy and Deputy Tate talked, Cassandra took a few moments to process her feelings and compose herself.

Andy said, "I'll drop you off here, and sit in at the sheriff's office while they talk to Nate."

"He doesn't have to talk to them, Andy," said Cassandra. "I hope Nate knows he can keep quiet or get a lawyer."

Chapter Sixteen

B ACK AT HER DESK, Cassandra remembered the last time she'd seen Devon and Nate in her office. They had mentioned Sam was behind on his rent and living expenses. She wondered if his student accounts were also delinquent?

If he was in dire straits financially, had Sam done something drastic to pay it off? It seemed far-fetched, but what if a bookie had sent out a henchman to hurt him?

Cassandra leaned closer to her computer screen, scrolling through Sam Soukup's college financial records. He hadn't qualified for federal financial aid; however, large scholarship payments had been deposited into his account each semester he'd been in school. She clicked on the name of the scholarship, but instead of seeing the expected description and account codes, she was met with something totally unfamiliar. Frowning, she switched tabs to an internet browser and began searching.

After a quarter of an hour had passed, she had yet to uncover any information on the Carson Future Leaders scholarship. Maybe it was funded locally by a service club like Sertoma or the VFW. The scholarship had been worth a significant amount of money, enough for tuition, books, room, and board. She checked Sam's academic records, as well, and noted his cumulative GPA was a 2.9. Hardly a straight-A student, but still decent grades overall. The scholarship must be awarded on a needs-based criterion. Current grades were kept in a different system and she couldn't see them. Safe to assume that if Sam's grades dropped significantly, he would have lost the scholarship.

What obligations did scholarship recipients have to the Future Leaders group? If it was a mentoring type of organization, it would be great if more students were able to apply and receive the assistance.

Perhaps that explained some of the roommate tension between Devon, Nate, and Sam. If Sam was receiving this large scholarship and still not paying his bills, his roommates had good reason to be upset. Where was the money going if not for room and board?

Cassandra's heart sank when she realized there would be no quick, easy answers to her questions. Sam was already gone and now Rhonda had to settle all his money issues in addition to mourning the loss of her child. She shut her laptop and shook her head.

She needed a change of scenery. When she grabbed her wallet and jacket, Murphy popped up from the little bed in the corner of her office where he'd been quietly snoring, and together they walked to the Student Center Coffee Shop. Inside, the line was short and the people-watching was a welcome distraction. She checked out the students studying or meeting at the small tables sprinkled in the seating area. At a large table, she recognized nearly all her student workers sitting together.

She wondered who was left in the main office if everyone was here. After getting her coffee, she approached the group. "Aloha! Are you folks just hanging out?"

"We're having our own little wake, Dr. Sato," Rachel sniffled, her eyes filled with sorrow. "We just got the news about Sam."

"I'm sorry, folks," Cassandra's heart tightened, the collective grief of the group hitting her like a wave. "I wish it had turned out differently." She pulled up a chair and joined their table.

"He's so young like us, and now he's gone," Rachel said. "It's a tragedy!"

"When people die unexpectedly, it's hard. It's good you're process-ing it together," Cassandra said.

"I feel bad that we weren't good friends." Rachel wiped under her eyes. "He kinda did his own thing, but maybe I should have tried harder to get to know him."

"I know how it feels to lose someone when you're young," said Cassandra. "My fiancé died when he was only twenty-six, and even though it was a long time ago, I still have days where I'm sad. It's normal to have mixed emotions."

Rachel cast a sideways glance at Devon. They'd only been dating a few months, but seemed like a good match. "Your fiancé?" said Rachel. "I'd just be a big puddle of tears forever."

"Even big losses get easier over time," Cassandra said.

Lance signed, *We just got out of our Death 101 class. Dr. Harris was helping us come up with ideas to figure out what really happened between Nate and Sam.*

Frowning, Cassandra signed and said, "I was at the play, too. We all saw what happened."

Cassandra sat back in her chair and observed the body language of the five students around the table. Rachel was the only one who looked genuinely teary. Devon sat next to her, his face slightly flushed, listening but preoccupied. Everyone else was somber and quiet.

Lance typed into his phone app and tapped a button so the automated male voice read his words. "Well, but there's some shady stuff about both of them. Look, I don't mean any disrespect, but Sam wasn't exactly a saint and it feels fake to act like it. Nate might be keeping something from us, too."

Devon shot to his feet. "Dude, those are my roommates you're talking about! We've been buddies for years. I'm telling you, it had to be an accident. Neither of them would do something like this." His voice wavered, and his eyes burned with unshed tears. "Sam's been gone for, what, a few hours? Maybe just—have some respect."

He grabbed his backpack and stomped away. Rachel called out after him, "Devon, wait!"

Rachel's expression looked like she didn't know whether to go after him. Cassandra shook her head. "Give him time to think," she advised. Cassandra glared at the others. "You know, Devon's got a point. I know you all want to help, but if you get in the middle of a police investigation, you could make things worse."

Rachel looked chagrined, but the other three seemed too interested in being involved to back off. Her break time was over, so Cassandra told the students bye and left with Murphy.

Before she crossed the doorway threshold, she heard a voice behind her, "We might have to dial back the Queen of Doom stuff in the office. She's scary for real."

It wasn't exactly a laughing matter, but the students still made her chuckle with their offbeat humor sometimes.

Stepping out of the student center to go back to her office, Cassandra nearly bumped into Simon Harris, who was wearing his leather jacket and an arrogant smirk. The hot coffee she was carrying sloshed out of the lid and burned her fingers. She gritted her teeth trying not to scream in pain.

Murphy scooted out of the way of their shoes and barked once. Then he nuzzled up to Harris's leg like a cat saying hello.

"Watch where you're going, Dr. Sato!" he said and pushed Murphy off his leg. "Control that animal."

She wouldn't mind if Murphy bit a chunk of flesh off his calf, but Murphy ignored Harris's gruff manner and sat next to Cassandra's foot, bowtie askew, a happy doggie grin on his white snout.

Cassandra wiped her hand on her scarf and took a deep breath. "I have a question about your Death 101 course, Simon."

"Oh? Consistently gets five star reviews on the rate your professors app!" His mouth settled into a smug smile.

Rolling her eyes, Cassandra pressed on. "The student workers from my office were discussing Sam and Nate's stage fight after your class, and they mentioned how you encouraged them to brainstorm possible scenarios to resolve it during your class lecture."

"So? I'm allowed to have an opinion," he said in a condescending tone.

"I'll ask you to do the same thing I told the students," Cassandra said. "Let the sheriff's department handle the investigation."

"Really? That's rich advice coming from you." Harris looked at Cassandra with disbelief. "You're the one who solved all three cases last semester. What, you don't want anyone else to steal your limelight? You think you're the only one worthy of being the center of attention?"

"That's not why I've helped the police," Cassandra said quickly.

"No matter what you say, I care about my students," Harris said firmly. "Injustice has to be answered, even if it's not your call to make. Good day, Cassandra." He nodded and went inside.

Steal my limelight? Cassandra fumed as she and Murphy walked along the large sidewalk around the quad. He had it all wrong. She wasn't involved because she loved attention. Supporting and advocating for students was her job. Was Simon heading to join the students' discussion in the coffee shop, or did he just happen to be walking that direction? The faculty senate wouldn't appreciate how carelessly he was teetering on the fine line of ethical behavior.

Her watch buzzed with a phone alert, and she clicked the talk button on her watch. It was Andy, saying he had been at the sheriff's office when Deputy Tate questioned Nate about the metal file. "I'm not a psychologist or anything, but I'd swear Nate seemed genuinely surprised to hear about the file being in his bag."

"What about fingerprints?" Cassandra asked, already dreading the answer.

"Tate said there were several partials, but the only clear ones were Shannon Bryant's. That makes sense, since it was his file." Andy paused, his voice sinking a bit. "We've confirmed that the whole stage crew had access to his tool bag and could've used items from it."

None of that information helped Nate.

"Has he said anything about Sam owing them money or whether he returned Sam's game system?"

"That's more complicated," Andy answered. "We had to give Nate time to recover after we told him Sam died this morning in the hospital." He hesitated. "He was adamant that he had no idea how the file ended up in his bag, and he held no grudges against Sam."

Cassandra sighed. "That's hard to believe."

"I've been reading through the students' statements again from the night of the play. Several people mentioned not seeing Nate before he hustled into place for the fight scene. When Deputy Tate questioned him, he never said anything about it."

"What if he just ran to the bathroom?"

"Then he shouldn't have anything to hide." Andy said, "They let Nate go home for now, but it doesn't look good for him. His story doesn't add up, and there's still the possibility that he might have placed the metal file there himself."

"Have you checked the security footage in the theater or around the Arts Center? Maybe it would show Nate and Sam before the fight began onstage?"

"Security footage," Andy chuckled. "It's been in my budget allocation request the past three years, but Dr. Gregory and the board of directors remove it every time. You know these guys won't spend an extra dime without a fight."

Cassandra hung up the phone, her mind recalculating every piece of information. Her gut said Nate was innocent, but she had no way of proving it.

When she returned to her office, she pulled up Sam's account again. The current interim president, Dr. Gregory, had been the former business office director and might have a few answers about the financial aid Sam had received.

Cassandra emailed Dr. Gregory the scholarship name and accounting code number and asked for more information about the application, due dates, and guidelines. She wrote, I HADN'T HEARD OF THIS CARSON FUTURE LEADERS SCHOLARSHIP BEFORE SEEING IT IN SAM SOUKUP'S FILE. IT'S VERY GENEROUS. I'D LIKE TO INFORM OTHER STUDENTS ABOUT IT TOO, SO THAT THEY CAN APPLY AS WELL. CAN YOU POINT ME IN THE RIGHT DIRECTION?

A few hours later, Dr. Gregory barged into her office and shut the door behind him. He pushed his hands into his pockets and fixed her with a stern gaze.

"Cassandra, snooping around in a student's financial records—a now *deceased* student's records—is a serious security breach. You shouldn't be looking at that file."

Wait, what? She blinked. He acted like she was in trouble for following up on a legitimate investigative lead. Checking Sam's financial situation was an obvious step in getting a better picture of his life before he died. Nevertheless, she kept her cool and heard him out as he continued to lecture her.

"I didn't reply to your email," he went on. "I'm going to assume you didn't know better and give you this advice in person: delete the email from your computer and hope it doesn't become part of any official investigation."

He flashed a stiff smirk and marched out of the office as quickly as he had come, leaving Cassandra stunned by his words.

Something about his tone must have alerted Murphy because he stood on his cushion, ears perked up, and his gaze shifted between the empty doorway and her.

She sat back in her chair. "What was that all about?"

Cassandra stewed over her encounters with Gregory and Harris. She wasn't afraid of productive conflict, but both conversations seemed especially heated. Could Harris be right that she was letting her ego take over? Was she taking on too much by herself when she should be leaving it to the professionals?

In an unprecedented display of affection, Murphy hopped into her lap. He must have sensed her mood. She scratched behind his ears and soaked in the cozy space, looking out the big window at the grass beginning to green in the quad.

Maybe Simon Harris had a point, but she'd been hired to connect with students and help out where possible. If so, then maybe she should try to find out as much as she could in an unofficial capacity.

The more Cassandra thought about it, the more convinced she became that she was headed on the right path. After all, who else would be able to use their insider knowledge of student behavior? She certainly hadn't seen Gregory or the sheriff asking the student workers about past problems or digging through financial records.

Packing up for the day, Cassandra and Murphy stepped out into the twilight. She would find out whatever there was to know about Sam Soukup's life both on and off campus.

Chapter Seventeen

T HE NEXT MORNING, NATE sat in Cassandra's office, wringing his hands anxiously. "I just can't stop feeling guilty about what happened to Sam," he said softly.

He looked like a hesitant deer, ready to bolt at the first sign of unease.

"You said it was an accident," Cassandra said in her most compassionate tone of voice. "Then it's not your fault. It's normal to feel a bunch of different emotions at the same time. Maybe it would help if you talk to a professional about this. Cinda Weller in the counseling office might help you sort through your feelings. But it will take time."

Nate nodded, too overwhelmed to speak. "I...I just have this feeling that something wasn't right," he continued. "I've gone over the last week a thousand times in my head. I swear to you, I didn't put the metal file in my backpack, and I don't know how the police found it there."

"Were you late on opening night? To the stage. Some of the kids said you weren't there."

At first his eyes were confused, but then recognition hit. "I couldn't find my rapier. I thought it was near my bag, but it wasn't. Took me a few minutes to find it. I made it to the scene in time. What's the big deal?"

"I don't know," she said. "The police have to go through their steps and follow the leads until they have more evidence. They're just doing their jobs," she encouraged. "Don't take it personally."

Cassandra handed him Cinda's phone number on scrap paper. "We're here to support you through this process. I can reach out to your professors and let them know you need to take a few days off. Can you follow up with them when you're feeling up to it?"

She was tempted to ask more about the investigation, but after yesterday's encounters with Harris and Gregory, she was extra careful to respect her professional boundaries.

"As long as you told the sheriff everything you can remember, hopefully they will gather more evidence to find out how the file got in your bag," Cassandra said. "You did tell them everything, right?"

Nate didn't meet her gaze. "Well, not every single meal we ate, or how many times Sam left the toothpaste tube uncovered in the bathroom the past week. But I told them all about the scene on the night of the play. Sam said something strange to me offstage before the fight. It was cryptic like, 'You'll be sorry.' He looked a little crazed, now that I think about it."

Knowing what Andy had said about the students' written statements and the interview with the deputy, Cassandra questioned if Nate was telling the truth.

She couldn't be perceived as taking sides. While she was checking into Sam's background, maybe she'd dig a little deeper into Nate's campus activities too. Someone knew more than they were telling.

After Nate left her office, Cassandra organized her notes and papers on her desk as she got ready for the budget work session, dreading having to face her boss Dr. Gregory, the bean counting zealot whose life purpose was reining in campus expenses.

When she looked up from her desk, Cinda was framed in her doorway dressed like Career Barbie with her wavy blonde hair tucked into a high ponytail. She wore black pants and shirt with a green blazer that matched her eyes and held a leather bound journal and a phone with the wallet attached to the back.

"Are you as excited about the budget meeting as me?" she drawled. Cinda had grown up as an Air Force brat and the Arkansas accent was the one that stuck.

"Can't wait," said Cassandra. "We have a few minutes, why don't you take a load off those heels."

They moved to sit in her comfy chairs in the sitting area of her office. Cassandra filled Cinda in on everything that had happened the last twenty-four hours. Just talking about it helped her feel a bit better and not like she had to solve every problem immediately. "I'm glad you stopped by early so we're on the same page now."

"Which page are we talking about?" Cinda frowned. "Your grant proposal with Shannon? Andy Summers has a girlfriend? Fischer acting weird during the president interviews? Or when you blubbered all over the pineapple upside down cake at your best friend's baby shower?"

"Thanks for providing the clarity. It's been a month." Cassandra stuck out her tongue. "When you're around, it's difficult to wallow in self pity."

"Part of my full-service friendship benefits," Cinda said. "FYI beginning tomorrow, we've scheduled some grief counselors in the Student Center for the rest of the week. Anyone who wants to drop in and talk will have the opportunity."

"Sam's passing makes me sad, no matter whose fault it is or whether it was just another random accident." Cassandra had been so focused on keeping the plates spinning in the air that she was glad Cinda had taken the initiative to set up the counseling. "I gave Nate Parker your phone number. He may be calling you to talk privately."

"We've provided grief counselors so often this year, we'll have to set up a permanent booth in the student center and hire special staff on retainer."

Cassandra groaned. "That's not funny."

"I'm not joking, sister."

When they stood up to head to the conference room for the next meeting, Cassandra's phone buzzed with a priority email. She paused to read the tersely worded note from the presidential search committee chairman, I REGRET TO INFORM YOU THAT OUR THIRD CANDIDATE WHO WAS SCHEDULED TO BEGIN INTERVIEWS THE END OF THIS WEEK HAS RETRACTED THEIR APPLICATION. THE COMMITTEE WILL CONVENE TO DISCUSS THE REMAINING CANDIDATES NEXT WEEK AS PLANNED. SINCERELY, TERRANCE ZIMMERMAN.

Cassandra looked at Cinda with a wry smile. "Our meeting just got a lot more interesting," She held her phone up so Cinda could read the news. "It really seems like the universe is trying to tell us something."

"I wasn't expecting the universe to have an opinion about our budget cuts," Cinda replied dryly.

"Oh, it has an opinion," said Cassandra. "But sometimes it takes a bit more finesse than usual to understand what it's saying. I have an idea. We could offer 'Hogwarts School of Witchcraft and Wizardry' weekend seminars! That'll bring some extra cash into the school."

"Or we could have a bake sale like the church ladies to raise extra money." Cinda shrugged and held out her arm like a medieval guard. "Let's go slay some dragons."

A failed presidential search was potentially catastrophic news, but dark humor and outrageous ideas were all Cassandra and Cinda had in their arsenal as they braced themselves for what was sure to be an emotionally draining afternoon.

Chapter Eighteen

W HEN CASSANDRA AND CINDA strutted into the meeting, ready to knock some sense into the undertaking, the boardroom was filled with an atmosphere of apprehensiveness. Yet before they could even begin the heart of their agenda, a tall woman with hair that seemed to droop on either side of her face went through an exhaustive list of every tiny step taken by the strategic steering committee. In excruciating detail.

After fifteen minutes, Cassandra eyed the sacrificial tray of colorful, frosted cookies with sprinkles sitting untouched on the center of the table. She fantasized about grabbing one and eating it for a sugar rush to stay awake, but then she remembered her father's words from when he coached her grade school softball team: *Sprinkles are for winners, honey.*

This group hadn't earned sprinkles.

"First item of business today is our tier one budget cuts." Dr. Gregory stood at the front of the boardroom next to a large white board with the financial projections for the next budget year neatly presented on a PowerPoint. "Has everyone had an opportunity to study the list? It's pretty obvious these enrollment numbers are too low. It's our job to get rid of the low-hanging fruit as quickly as possible."

Cassandra guessed the faculty and students in the Physics and European Studies departments wouldn't appreciate their subject areas being compared to a sagging apple tree.

Her irritation with the number crunchers had been slowly bubbling over since her days as Dean of Students. She had no respect for those who dismissed students as constituents, or college programs as nothing more than pawns to be sacrificed at the first sign of hard times. And it was totally beyond her how anyone could ignore the endearing quirks of each struggling student and chronically under-funded department.

The graph showed tier one consisted of eliminating majors and courses with low enrollment, delaying all vehicle and technology purchases until the next president was named, and limiting out-of-state travel.

Cassandra wanted more specifics, but waited for others on the advisory committee to speak up first. Bob Soukup watched Dr. Gregory's presentation, his eyes fixed on the whiteboard with a fierce determination. Cassandra felt a pang of sadness for the man who had lost his grandson just the day before. She wondered if he was in denial, trying to distract himself from his grief by focusing on something tangible. But as the meeting wore on, and Bob contributed to the discussion with conviction and vigor about finding solutions to their financial crisis, she had to assume that this was his way of coping. Though she admired his resilience, she couldn't avoid thinking his priorities were misplaced.

As she looked around the room, Cassandra found herself wondering if anyone else felt the same way. Some nodded in agreement, while others stared ahead silently as if they hadn't even noticed Bob's attendance. For Cassandra, it was a moment of silent reflection; a reminder that sometimes all you can do is take a deep breath, let go, and mourn.

Cassandra glanced to her left where the interim financial aid manager was perched on the edge of his chair. On her right sat the Assistant Director of Student Affairs, who looked like he had been the same age for the past twenty years. She could barely make out a glimpse of his balding head, which was bent so low that it almost touched his phone as he furiously typed away on Words With Friends. A ferocious battle must have been taking place, because he didn't even flinch at any of the conversations happening around him.

"Exactly which low enrollment courses do you propose cutting?" A faculty member from the European Studies department asked while making air quotes around the words low enrollment.

"Physics 425, Art History 373, and Anthropology 361, which is the Death 101 course." Gregory rested a finger on his notes, "This is part of cutting the Gerontology department."

With the aging Baby Boomer population—of which Gregory, Soukup, and her officemate were clearly members—wouldn't it make more sense to keep the Gerontology department open to prepare students for future careers in those fields? The words screamed in her head, and she waited for them to quiet to a rumble before opening her mouth and speaking calmly. "Isn't the future growth of Gerontology one of the hottest employment sectors?"

The European Studies professor added, "If you eliminate the major, then students who want to study that topic will have to take those courses as electives."

Before anyone could talk over her, Cassandra said, "Perhaps we should be building bridges between departments so that these courses count for several majors instead of cutting them off? We could try it on a temporary basis and measure whether enrollment rises. Restructuring might justify keeping the courses, even if we have to combine some majors."

Gregory's eyes squinted, and his tone was condescending. "We need to remove the outliers. Stick to the meat and potatoes of the main curriculum. Morton is a small, private college. We have no need for unnecessary, frilly courses."

The faculty member frowned. "A true liberal arts education is well rounded and encompasses more than just the basic core subjects. Perhaps Dr. Sato has a point. I'd be willing to look at ways to integrate these courses into more departments."

Soukup scoffed. "This has been a long time coming. All of our attempts to dodge the inevitable have blown up in our faces. We have no other choice but to start slashing the budget. I don't take pleasure in this, but it has to be done. If you're not going to cut those classes, we'll just have to find another way." He looked at Cassandra, "What's your department, miss?"

Bob Soukup one-hundred-percent knew who Cassandra was and where she worked, but he'd rather play games. She was thirty-four-years-old, and he just called her "miss" as if she were a teenager. Reminding herself that he was grieving, she clamped her mouth shut to stop herself from snapping at him. With a tight smile, she replied, "Student Affairs, Mr. Soukup."

"Aren't you the people who host those awful movies in the student center and waste money on extracurricular clubs like knitting and squirrel feeding?"

Every higher ed institution she'd seen had similar conflicts between the money people, the academics, and student life folks like herself. Looking around the table, it seemed like a war among the generations. The geezers seemed to think the college was a soulless factory where you start with empty-headed freshmen and output graduates in the most cost-effective, efficient manner possible. In Cassandra's humble opinion, most student learning occurred outside the classroom where they learned the softer skills like leadership, time management, and social skills.

Dr. Zimmerman interrupted, "Let's not get derailed here. Our Biology department has ancient laptops that need replacing, and the chemistry labs haven't been updated in four years. What's included in this line item for vehicle and technology purchases? My budget request was approved last fall, but where's the money on your spreadsheet?"

Gregory said, "Things have changed since last fall. Obviously. The strategic steering committee felt that all larger purchases are best postponed until the new president is onboard. That person may want to establish different priorities."

Zimmerman's face turned red, and he stuttered, "B-but we've already ordered the machines!"

"Then cancel the order," Gregory said. "You acted prematurely and without authorization."

"I had assurances from Dr. Nielson."

"Dr. Nielson isn't here anymore."

Zimmerman rocked back in his chair like Gregory had physically struck him. Murmurs buzzed around the table, and people flipped through the documents in front of them, most likely searching for their own pet projects.

A thought occurred to Cassandra. "Excuse me. Dr. Gregory, when you said, 'all larger purchases,' what exactly did you mean?"

"Seems pretty simple to me, Dr. Sato. All purchases of vehicles and technology are on hold until the new president is in place and approves them." He shrugged.

She and Shannon Bryant had poured hours of work into their grant application package. Her stomach sunk. "The matching funds for the emergency management software system grant aren't in that category, are they?"

Gregory stared at her and annunciated each syllable, "Nothing will be authorized until the new president is hired."

"But the grant application closes next week. They won't award us if the college refuses to fund our share."

"It's out of my hands," Gregory put his palms up. "No extra expenditures."

God help her, she battled to keep her voice under control. She shot up from her seat and leaned her entire torso over the table. "That's why we're applying for the grant! Why would you cancel the one thing that's going to earn us money?"

The whispering died down and fifteen sets of eyeballs landed on her. She had dared to raise her voice at the old curmudgeon.

Gregory scowled, "Because it's still going to cost us money up front. I'm being fiscally responsible. We don't need all the latest fancy equipment."

"Need I remind you of the student protests only four months ago? Those happened because we didn't have the right equipment. We narrowly escaped being sued by the injured student's parents. Next time, we might not get off so easily, and it could end up costing the college much more than a new emergency management system."

Her cheeks hot, Cassandra picked up her glass with a shaky hand and took a long sip of cool water. It didn't dampen the frustration seething inside.

Just then a hard knock on the closed wooden door sounded and in walked Simon Harris. Cassandra blinked for a few moments, sat in her chair, and the word dapper popped into her head. Harris approached the head of the conference table wearing a light brown tweed suit, bow tie, and brown, rimmed glasses. His costume was exactly the opposite of Harris's normal jeans and battered brown leather jacket.

She glanced to his belt, only mildly surprised not to see an Indiana Jones style whip coiled on his hip.

"This is a closed meeting, Dr. Harris," Gregory scolded.

"Because you cowards are afraid to have this discussion in front of the campus community, I'm sure," Harris said. "You plot in secret, and none of you has to claim responsibility later for cutting our programs and funds. This witch-hunt is a travesty."

"Which program are you concerned about? Anthropology isn't on the tier one list."

"No, but the Theater department was mentioned, as was my very popular course, Death 101."

"We've gone over this already, and your course is an elective," Gregory said. "We've no space in our course catalog for frivolous electives. Students in their late teens and early twenties have no need to discuss a morbid topic like death when there are more relevant courses available."

"Frivolous! Topics in the Death 101 syllabus are critical for pre-health and human service majors alike." Harris stood several places away from where Cassandra was seated, but the bulging vein in his temple was apparent even from this distance. He said, "Estate planning, insurance issues—all of it needs to be discussed. That makes it one of the most useful courses we offer here, whether you're a student or edging up to your grave." He glowered at them.

Cassandra coughed.

Gregory scowled near his whiteboard while at the other end of the table Soukup crossed his arms in front of his chest, his face ashen.

Harris seemed to notice Soukup for the first time and cleared his throat. "Bob, I'm truly sorry for your loss." After a moment of awkward silence, Harris softened his tone. "The Board of Directors has final approval, no matter what your committee recommends today. I'll show up at the next board meeting with a crowd of students. It will never pass."

Gregory pressed the forward button on his PowerPoint presentation. "Moving on..." He glanced meaningfully at Harris. "You can read our recommendations once they're completed." Gregory continued, "As you can see there are three departments which have had declining enrollment for years. Our steering committee proposes we move the core courses from Gerontology into the Social Work department. But the Theatre department is hemorrhaging money. They've already cut back to two smaller shows in the fall and one large production in the spring, but it hasn't resulted in the cost savings we'd anticipated. It's time we just eliminate it."

Bob Soukup barked from the end of the boardroom table, "Axe it? My grandson isn't even in the ground yet, and you're already trying to scrap the whole department? I won't stand for it."

"Bob, the entire campus community is sorry and our thoughts are with your family at this difficult time. No disrespect intended, but you have to admit the arts are simply a nice addition to life. Like frosting on a cupcake. But they aren't the main meal." Gregory's tone was condescending, even for him. "When you're in a financial position such as Morton's, you have to stick to meat and potatoes. Maybe a student club could manage one of the productions with volunteers as directors and staff?"

Harris's eyes widened so big that if he had been a cartoon character, they would have popped out of his face. Cassandra's head swung back and forth watching the exchange like a tennis match.

"As the faculty sponsor for the spring play, I'm already paid so little I'm practically a volunteer," Harris spluttered. "Same goes for our choreography and combat directors. There's one full-time office manager who wears so many hats, even I don't know all what she does to keep the place afloat." Harris's voice grew louder as he became more passionate. Maybe drama was more his style than Cassandra had previously realized. "Morton College's theater department benefits the entire Carson community. Do you think another organization in town could pull off these high-quality performances?"

Soukup chimed in from the end of the table. "Harris is right on this one. Soukup Enterprises has been sponsoring plays for years, but you can't expect five-star performances with a ragtag bunch of volunteers!"

"Our costume closet alone is worth thousands of dollars." Harris pressed both palms on the tabletop. "Nearby high schools pay us to rent costumes for their plays. If you close the theater department, you'll lose that revenue source, not to mention the connections and goodwill associated with it."

Gregory rose from his seat. "My statistics show the box office ticket sales are far too low to cover the annual expenses. In order for the plays to continue, the program needs to find more avenues of self support," he said confidently.

"It's not coming out of your own damn pocket, Bob," grumbled Soukup.

His gruff personality clashed sharply with Gregory's composed and articulate demeanor. Cassandra couldn't help but think they were two grumpy old men.

Soukup said, "The theater department cuts are off the table. Understood?"

Both Bobs seemed to be on a collision course as they locked eyes, Soukup's gaze unflinching despite Gregory's red-rimmed orbs, and the former's nose swollen from years of drinking. Couldn't the Bobs just stop talking and retire already?

"I'm just saying, I can't prop up this college forever." Soukup stood and pointed at Gregory. "You're going to have to do something big if you want to boost enrollment and keep this ship afloat. Choose your new president wisely, or Carson will become yet another forgotten backwater."

And with those words ringing in their ears, Soukup made an exit worthy of any theatrics stage as he stormed out of the room.

Chapter Nineteen

Returning to her office after the budget meeting debacle, Cassandra needed a quiet break from the chaos. She shut her door, heated a cup of green tea in her Keurig, and chose an instrumental playlist from her phone's music app. Resting on the couch, she set her phone alarm for ten minutes and closed her eyes for a mindfulness practice but found herself almost immediately overwhelmed with thought.

Sam's death weighed heavily on her heart because it seemed so avoidable. The accusations against Nate and the potential budget cuts were a reminder of how powerless she was in this situation, while fear of coming up empty in the presidential search loomed as a possibility.

A heavy exhaustion weighed down her chest as anger spiked within her at the unfairness of it all. Soon, however, she realized that yet again her thoughts had strayed from counting breaths.

She tapped off her timer with four minutes still remaining. "I give up," she sighed. "Let's roll."

Murphy's furry head popped up, anticipating his imminent leash hookup, sensing Cassandra's need for movement and change of scenery. As they trotted down to the Arts Center, Cassandra acknowledged that counting breaths would not be enough this time. Maybe this new location would set something inside of her free.

The classrooms were busy and lively, yet the lobby was oddly empty. She meandered to the main auditorium and found it dimly lit by several spotlights casting soft circles of light onto its stage.

Gently tugging on the leash, she guided Murphy back to where she'd originally been sitting the night of the play and settled in the darkness to rehash all the somber moments. For once, Murphy cooperated and lay peacefully in her lap, letting her rub the soft hair of his head. When she'd first taken him in months ago, he'd snarled and snapped at her fingers. Poor little guy, she thought, he probably still missed his owner, the former Morton President Deborah Winters.

Thinking about President Winters and Sam soon led to remembering the last hike she and Paul took before he got sick. Sitting side-by-side in the narrow meadow atop Olomana. The taste of egg salad on wheat bread still lingered in her mouth. When their gazes met, she felt a warmth forming in her chest. Around them, the ground fell away down the steep sides of the peak. Toward the ocean, Honolulu stretched out before them.

As they munched egg sandwiches overlooking a lush tropical valley, he'd said, "I can't imagine ever leaving here."

"You know my career path. Are you saying we can't move to the mainland when I get a better job?" She'd asked him this before, but it seemed like a never-ending discussion.

Suddenly, loud voices echoed from backstage. Two men and a woman were arguing about something. Her voice sounded familiar.

"Firing Dr. Bryant is so unfair!"

"They'll probably cancel the whole play now that they're axing the theater department," said the woman. "All that work for nothing!"

"Kinda dramatic there, eh?"

The woman came into Cassandra's view on the left side of the stage. Sela Roberts' voice carried into the seats. "I say we plan another protest!"

"It worked once, but I doubt they'd listen to us again," one of the guys countered.

Cassandra's hand froze on Murphy's back as she processed what they were saying. It sounded like they already knew the theater department was on the budget chopping block. Well, there was only one person who would have leaked news from a private meeting – Simon Harris.

The kids were in an uproar, but they had to be mistaken about Shannon Bryant being fired. She would be one of the first to know if that was true.

Cassandra's body tensed, and her hand froze on Murphy's back. She'd heard that animals sensed the feelings of the surrounding people, and sure enough he stood on his hind legs, propped his front paws on the seat in front of her, and barked.

"Shhh, Murphy," she tried to move him, but he growled, and she dropped her hands worried he'd take his feelings out on her.

One of the guys stepped to the front of the stage and held his hand up to shield his eyes from the spotlight. "Who's there!" He demanded.

Cassandra stood and moved forward until the light revealed her face to the students.

"Dr. Sato! What are you doing here?"

"Did I hear you folks talking about Dr. Bryant?"

A guy wearing a Red Sox baseball cap said, "He didn't show up for our Deaf Studies class this morning. His TA came in and told us Dr. Bryant was suspended pending a college investigation."

"It's probably just a formality," Cassandra kept her voice neutral. "I don't know any more than you do about the allegations against him. Please don't do anything rash until we know more." She shrugged and checked for messages on her phone before adding, "At least that's my take on it."

Academic politics were her concern, however, and it looked like the budget battle over the theater department would have to move down her priority list. First, she needed to fight to help her friend Shannon Bryant keep his job.

This had Interim President Gregory's fingerprints all over it. Blaming Bryant for Sam's death would make it easier for him to discredit the entire department and justify his draconian budget cuts.

"We're planning a memorial service for Sam," said the Red Sox guy. "Sela's working on the display, and Professor Harris said we could use some props from the play."

"A few people went to Sam's apartment to box up his things for his mom," Sela said.

"That's really thoughtful of you," Cassandra said, "I'm sorry you lost your friend, but I bet his mom will appreciate your help."

Murphy ducked up the side stairway and trotted over to Sela, his leash trailing behind him. She scooped him up and crooned in her

Caribbean island British accent, "What a handsome boy," then buried her face in his furry side and petted him.

Cassandra had long since gotten over how friendly Murphy was to people who welcomed his affection versus how grumpy he could be around her. Obviously, the students needed all the compassion they could get when they were going through a difficult loss.

Cassandra watched as the students draped the stage with black curtains and arranged a pair of leather boots, a hat, and a bandit's coat on white fabric in the middle of the stage. Sela added a flower bouquet and a picture of Sam.

Sela stepped to the edge near Cassandra, "Do you think we can still save the play? We haven't had a chance to perform it yet."

The others hung their heads in silence, the uncertainty of the situation consuming them. Cassandra scanned their faces and could feel the weight of their doubt. She wished she could do something to comfort them, but her responsibilities held her back.

"I see how much this means to you and the department," she said gently. "It'll take some time to sort everything out with the college. Let's take a break for now. I'll make sure to follow up on Dr. Bryant's status as soon as possible."

The students hesitantly shuffled out of the auditorium as Cassandra thanked them for their hard work and dedication.

She had so many plans; ambitions that would provide for more than just her own family. Establishing her reputation and academic credentials took time, and the way things had worked out, Cassandra didn't have children of her own. But at Morton she was responsible for the well-being of several thousand young adults.

And right now, a group of them were in crisis.

Murphy barked twice from his spot onstage, where he had been quietly watching the students. Taking a deep breath, Cassandra slowly released it, summoning the determination that fueled her to move four thousand miles from her island home: "C'mon Murph, let's see what kind of hunt the vultures are planning now."

Chapter Twenty

D R. GREGORY HAD BEEN a thorn in Cassandra's side since she first arrived at Morton College. He imposed a hiring freeze, leaving her team of student workers to do the executive assistant's job in her office. He was the bean counter in chief of denying her matching funds for the text-based emergency management system. And he was a condescending jerk in meetings. It was time someone called him out for going too far.

Cassandra waved at his assistant Julie as she approached the open door of President Gregory's office. "Is now an okay time?"

Cassandra's face must have shown her frustration because Julie's eyes widened, and she looked nonplussed. "Of course, Dr. Sato."

Cassandra eased the door closed behind her before marching into Gregory's office. She crossed her arms and scowled, her voice tight with accusation. "I hear you suspended Shannon Bryant without conferring with the leadership team first?"

Gregory leaned back in his chair, hands clasped behind his head as he coldly laid out the rationale for his decision. He refused to divulge details as it was a confidential personnel matter and lectured Cassandra on the academic reasons why Bryant's job was on the line. They had even already consulted with the college attorney about the case.

Gregory spoke with an air of superiority, "As you are aware, our code of conduct is stringent in order for faculty to be good examples to students. The campus security report pointed out that Dr. Bryant failed to conduct the required safety check on opening night of *The Three Musketeers.*"

Cassandra understood that, but hadn't realized Gregory had even read the file. "But how can we be certain a safety check would have shown that Nate's sword was tampered with? There could be other contributing factors in the accident. Shannon Bryant is a respected member of our campus community. We can't lose a good professor because we're looking for a scapegoat."

Gregory simply shrugged and shifted his attention to outside the window. "Once he was arrested, I saw fit for us to conduct our own internal inquiry of Shannon Bryant's involvement."

Cassandra glared at his unyielding profile for several heartbeats before uttering one word. "Arrested?"

The corners of Gregory's mouth twitched upwards slightly in dark pleasure over her surprise.

"This has gone way too far," she snapped before turning on her heel and storming out of his office.

He was kidding himself if he thought she'd give up so easily.

She decided to leave her car in the parking lot and set off walking toward Main Street and the sheriff's office. Maybe the extra time would help her temper cool down before she saw Sheriff Hart or Deputy Tate.

Her one mission was to get answers.

She walked past the Gas and Sweets and The Home Team bar, the warm sun on her back. In front of Ron's Pawn store, she noticed a familiar face. Terrance Zimmerman stepped out of the sheriff's office, adjusting his glasses. "Hey, Cassandra," he said. "I came as soon as I heard to check on Shannon. I'm expecting to hear back from the union rep. If they hold him overnight, the faculty senate will write a letter to the newspaper."

"I'm glad he has your support. President Gregory suspended Bryant pending an internal investigation," Cassandra told him. "What the heck are these people thinking?"

"It gets worse," Terrance warned as he stepped closer. "I also received word from our accreditation liaison contact that Morton is under investigation for the altercation at the play. Apparently, they are concerned about the high number of incidents that have occurred at Morton recently and are considering placing the college on their watch list."

The accreditation agency wasn't the only one concerned about the incidents, but the watch list? Cassandra took a big inhale to keep herself from rolling her eyes. "Do you really think our accreditation is at risk over a sword fight? Some of those previous incidents were outside of our control. Surely the committee would understand?"

"They are not in the habit of making exceptions. Oh, and one other thing, ..." He lowered his voice. "I believe it would be prudent to mention that I saw Marcus Fischer meeting with Fran Morrison yesterday at the field house, which I found highly irregular for a presidential candidate."

That was odd, indeed. Her initial instinct that Fischer and Morrison had hit it off must have been correct. Her stomach clenched. When she opened her mouth, nothing came out for a few seconds. "I appreciate you letting me know, Terrance. I'll follow up with him about that later."

Zimmerman hopped into his Prius and drove off.

Cassandra paused to assimilate everything he'd just said.

First off, she had to put aside her personal misgivings about Fischer and Morrison, because the college took priority. Being linked to an accreditation watch list fiasco would be a career killer, one sure to obliterate any future hope of advancement. It'd be like having the accrediting agency officially dub her the Queen of Doom!

Meg O'Brien's car pulled into the spot the Prius had just vacated. Meg awkwardly exited the car, beach ball sized stomach leading the way as she swung herself onto the sidewalk. "Hey you." They side hugged. "Are you here because of Shannon?"

"This is crazy." Cassandra said, "Gregory suspended Shannon from his teaching position. Terrance thinks Morton's accreditation is on the line. And Fischer and Morrison had some kind of powwow at the field house."

Meg groaned, "Geez, I'm just here for Shannon. Promise me you won't murder Fischer so I don't have to come back and bail your butt out."

Cassandra rolled her eyes and smiled. "Not funny, but I love you for trying."

They stepped into the sheriff's office which looked more like an outpost than a full-service police station. There was a reception area, an officer's desk, and a conference room for meetings. The deputy informed them Shannon was in custody, but couldn't confirm what he did that got him arrested.

"Can I see him?" Cassandra asked.

The young deputy stared back at her with an impassive expression. "Everything is still under investigation," he finally replied with a canned phrase. "Sheriff Hart will give more information when it's available."

As Cassandra peeked through the doorway of the meeting room, she spied Shannon Bryant sitting alone at the wood conference table with a pad of legal paper and a bottle of water in front of him.

He looked up at her and made a slight wave. *Don't worry, I'm fine*, he signed. *Waiting for my lawyer.*

Sheriff Hart's eyes lit up when he saw Meg. "Ah! Here you are! Our own local interpreter. Now we don't need to wait any longer."

Meg quickly shook her head and signed while she spoke so that Shannon could see her from where he sat. "No, I'm just here for a little while, until your licensed legal interpreter arrives. I have a conflict of interest. I can't interpret the police interview with Dr. Bryant. Not only are we coworkers at Morton College, he's my friend."

He eyed Meg skeptically, "Don't you have some confidential oath like a doctor to 'do no harm,' or some technical loophole like that?"

"Well, I follow a code of conduct," said Meg. "If we were in the hospital emergency room, I would interpret for anyone to help save their life. This isn't a life or death situation, but it's still serious and has big consequences, so you need someone neutral who understands the legalese and procedures. I agreed to be here while you processed him, but you need someone else for your interviews."

Sheriff Hart's neck flushed crimson as he fumed about wasted time and cash. Cassandra had a gut feeling Dr. Gregory was pulling the strings in this fiasco. She signed slowly and carefully while she told the Sheriff, "I believe Shannon. Trust me, he would never hurt a student. "

Instead of looking grateful for her help, Bryant frowned and he signed, *Stay out of it! How dare you assume you can speak for me.*

"I didn't say --"

I mean it. Leave. Bryant broke eye contact, unscrewed his water bottle, and took a long drink, ignoring Cassandra.

Before Cassandra could respond, Meg gave her a firm nudge and mouthed the word, *'Go'.* With an ache of confusion and betrayal, she followed Meg's advice and left the station.

As she trudged back to campus, her steps were heavy with self recrimination. Shannon's rejection had thrown a monkey wrench into her plans, and she couldn't find any comfort in pretending Fischer and Dr. Morrison were working out together at the field house. She thought hard to come up with any sort of plausible excuse for the presence of a search committee member and a candidate for the president position being in the same place. But she came up with a big, fat goose egg.

Distrust wormed its way insidiously into her already fragile feelings about their relationship. She'd watch Fischer more closely, and if he made any missteps, she'd run for the door. There was too much at stake to give her heart to someone who didn't deserve it.

She'd rather be alone the rest of her life than ride a drama train of relationship ups and downs.

Chapter Twenty-One

B Y THE TIME CASSANDRA arrived in her office, her back was slightly sweaty from the afternoon sun, and Murphy had had plenty of time to do his business. A whole boatload of uncomfortable thoughts had settled in. She'd meant well when she offered to help Shannon at the station. Now her conscience was prickling as she remembered his angry response. It seemed the consequences for helping her new friend would be more than she expected.

At her desktop computer, she answered some emails and found one from her contact with the technology grant foundation. The simple auto-generated statement said, YOUR GRANT APPLICATION WAS SUCCESSFULLY SUBMITTED. DECISIONS WILL BE MADE IN SIX TO EIGHT WEEKS, AND YOU WILL BE NOTIFIED BY EMAIL.

Warm pleasure at seeing the words "successfully submitted" spread throughout her chest. She looked up and said a quiet prayer of thanks. Among a crappy week, finally a bright spot.

Which lasted less than two minutes, until she remembered the budget cuts meeting where Gregory promised to withhold the college matching funds.

She opened the budget cuts PowerPoint document that Dr. Gregory had shared with the committee. The numbers were dire, but she had to hope that the board of directors would understand that the grant was an overall budget win even though the college would have to match some funds. Bottom line, they'd still be ahead a couple hundred thousand dollars and have a brand new emergency management system.

Wasn't it a no-brainer?

As the discussion replayed through her head, she felt her blood pressure rising at the condescending way Gregory had told her it was non-negotiable. Other people supposedly smarter and more important than herself had decided already. Also, how Bob Soukup had called her "Miss."

Suddenly, her hypocrisy hit her like a coconut falling from a tree. As a young adult and a minority woman, people often underestimated Cassandra. Or tried to take over and decide things for her, thinking she wasn't capable of doing it herself.

And she had done the exact same thing to Shannon. She was treating him differently because he was deaf. Worse, she assumed the Sheriff wouldn't listen to him because he was disabled.

However one takeaway she'd learned from knowing Shannon, besides some conversational sign language, was he didn't seem disabled in any of the ways that mattered. He was smart, accomplished, and wholly capable.

No wonder he'd gotten mad.

She made a frantic call to the sheriff's station just in time to hear that Shannon had been released. Without hesitation, Cassandra leashed Murphy and set out across campus, determined to make things right.

Cassandra pressed on Shannon Bryant's doorbell light button, expecting the dark office to be empty, but was surprised when he answered. He seemed resigned to his fate, stacking books and packing documents into a cardboard box.

Shannon's normally friendly face looked drawn and tired. *It's too late*, he signed. *Gregory decided. They canceled my contract.*

Cassandra felt her anger bubbling up again and gritted her teeth to suppress it. She wanted to shout, but it wouldn't do any good now.

She didn't trust her ASL skills for this difficult conversation, so she pulled out her phone and spoke a message into her notes microphone. I KNEW NOTHING ABOUT THE SUSPENSION UNTIL YOU WERE ARRESTED. THE SHERIFF LET YOU GO FAST.

They didn't have enough evidence to keep me. He made a faint smile and shrugged. *Doesn't matter, results the same*, he signed. Shannon shook his head sadly. IT'S NOT JUST ABOUT THE SUSPENSION, he typed on his phone. I'VE BEEN CONSIDERING A MOVE FOR SOME TIME NOW. He paused, gathering his thoughts before continuing. MY DAUGHTER LIVES WITH HER MOTHER IN OMAHA AND I ... WELL, ... MAYBE THIS IS A SIGN THAT I SHOULD MOVE CLOSER TO THEM.

Cassandra understood his ambivalence. She didn't know him well enough to have an opinion on whether he was using the timing of this as an excuse to do what he already wanted to do anyway, or if he was just hiding.

"I see," she mumbled, not sure how else to respond in such an emotional moment. She hesitated for a few moments before gathering her courage. BUT WHAT ABOUT YOUR LIFE HERE AT MORTON COLLEGE, she said, choosing her words carefully so as not to offend him or upset him further, but still make her point clearly. I CAME TO TELL YOU OUR GRANT APPLICATION WAS ACCEPTED. WE FIND OUT IN SIX TO EIGHT WEEKS WHETHER THEY AWARD US THE MONEY. DON'T LET GREGORY WIN. FIGHT FOR YOUR JOB IF THAT'S WHAT YOU REALLY WANT.

Shannon shook his head and tapped on his phone, I CAN'T, he wrote. MY DAUGHTER AND EX-WIFE ARE IN OMAHA. He met her gaze. THE MEDIA ATTENTION WOULD BE TOO MUCH FOR THEM IF I FOUGHT THIS.

Cassandra could understand why he didn't want to put those closest to him in the line of fire. She had always appreciated how Shannon viewed teaching as a way to help others learn about his culture and language rather than simply a job to pay the bills. He was a role model to so many students that it would be a shame for him to leave like this.

WHAT IF YOU PUBLICLY EXPLAIN THAT IT WAS A HORRIBLE TRAGEDY THAT NO ONE COULD HAVE FORESEEN AND MAKE A CASE FOR WHY YOU SHOULD BE ABLE TO KEEP YOUR JOB? she asked, her voice rising with excitement as she realized this might be possible after all. YOU CAN USE YOUR OWN EXPERIENCE AS AN EXAMPLE OF WHY EDUCATORS SHOULD TAKE SAFETY SERIOUSLY WHEN IT COMES TO THEATRICAL PERFORMANCES.

Bryant's face reddened, and she thought he was going to yell at her again. He seemed to deliberate whether he wanted to tell her more, then took a deep breath and reached a decision.

His fingers danced across his smartphone as he typed out a long paragraph. AT MY PREVIOUS POST, I HAD A RELATIONSHIP WITH ONE OF THE GRADUATE STUDENTS. THE BIGWIGS ACCUSED ME OF UNPROFESSIONAL CONDUCT, AND I HAD TO LEAVE THE POSITION QUIETLY. MY EX AND I DON'T LIVE

TOGETHER ANYMORE, BUT I RESPECT HER TOO MUCH TO SEE HER NAME IN THE PAPERS BECAUSE OF OUR IMPULSIVENESS FIFTEEN YEARS AGO.

Are you saying you married your grad student?

Shannon nodded. WE DID. BUT UNDERSTAND, I AM PARTLY RESPONSIBLE FOR SAM'S DEATH. MAYBE, IF I HAD INSISTED ON THE SAFETY CHECK BEFORE OUR WARM-UP THAT NIGHT, WE COULD HAVE AVERTED THIS WHOLE TRAGEDY. I ACCEPT MY GUILT AND TAKE OWNERSHIP OF THE CONSEQUENCES.

Cassandra sighed, feeling a wave of sympathy wash over her. Nothing about this situation was simple. She could understand why Shannon had been so reluctant to fight Gregory's decision, and why he wanted to keep his past mistakes where they belonged. Still, she knew that someone of Shannon's caliber was too valuable for Morton College to lose without a fight.

I'm sorry about what I said at the police station, she signed. *I wasn't trying to speak for you because I'm hearing and you're deaf. I'm standing behind you because you're my coworker and friend.*

It was a subtle distinction, but one she hoped translated properly into ASL.

AND I'M SORRY ABOUT WHAT HAPPENED AT YOUR FORMER JOB, she spoke into her phone. BUT YOU HAVE DONE NOTHING WRONG HERE AT MORTON COLLEGE, AND THE STUDENT'S DEATH SHOULDN'T BE USED AS AN EXCUSE FOR THEM TO FIRE YOU. MAYBE YOU DON'T HAVE TO FIGHT ALONE.

The little muscle in his cheek pulsing like a heartbeat was the only indication he gave as he gathered his thoughts. *I don't need you.*

Cassandra looked slightly down and nodded. *I know*, she signed.

But, thank you. Friend. His bear-sized hand squeezed her shoulder and when their eyes met, hers teared up with emotion.

Perhaps making his plight public wasn't the way out of this mess. Cassandra needed a plan, one that promised stealth and success. She had been born under the sign of the ox, and she was loyal. Always.

Chapter Twenty-Two

RESTLESS FROM HER TALK with Shannon, Cassandra decided to grab a snack and a latte from the Student Center. As she was making her way inside, Murphy barked at someone sitting alone on a metal bench. Cassandra had nearly walked past Rhonda Soukup, her face drawn and pale, quietly drinking from a disposable coffee cup. Cassandra cautiously walked over to see if she wanted some company.

Rhonda had a small smile on her face as she spoke, "My shop is closed today, thought I'd check out the competition. Not bad."

Murphy nuzzled his head against her ankles and when Rhonda scratched him behind the ears he put his paws up on her knee looking for more attention.

Rhonda scooted over to make room for Murphy. After a few minutes of petting him sweetly, Cassandra drifted the conversation closer to what was on her mind since leaving Gregory's office yesterday.

Cassandra cleared her throat nervously,"Um, do you mind if we talk about Sam."

Rhonda stayed quiet for several moments before finally responding in an emotional voice, "What about him?"

Cassandra gave Rhonda an anxious look before continuing, "Well... I ran into some of his classmates today and they were packing up his stuff from his apartment with your permission.... Is that true?"

"I just couldn't bring myself to do it," she confessed. "You know, Sam was a mess before the play. He was terrified of embarrassing himself in front of the audience, so it was really nice when those kids stepped up to help."

Cassandra remembered how Rhonda had told her about moving Sam from his hometown for most of his childhood in order to keep him away from bad influences.

"Any chance he ever got into drugs or anything like that?" Cassandra asked, her voice tight as she mentioned the dreaded subject. "Or did he talk about gambling?"

"The police already asked me that," Rhonda said quietly. "He never told me much about his school life, but I think I would have known if he'd been using drugs. I suppose his roommates would know that."

If Devon or Nate had told the police about those things, no one had passed that detail along to Cassandra yet.

"Did you know anything about the scholarship Sam won?" She asked Rhonda cautiously.

Rhonda shook her head sadly and wiped away tears. "Nope, he never mentioned it to me," she sniffled. "I practically begged him to apply for financial aid and he kept saying no."

Cassandra felt for Rhonda, it had to be rough being a parent, wanting to give your child space but never knowing if they were making responsible choices.

"Then one day, there it was on the kitchen table: an acceptance letter for a scholarship! I cooked up his favorite dinner, macaroni and cheese to celebrate. Knowing that all we'd have to worry about was basic support instead of those crazy student loans while he earned his degree. When I read it, I was over the moon."

"It changed everything," Rhonda whispered, blowing her nose loudly into a tissue. "If only he'd lived long enough..." She trailed off, then asked quietly, "Is it true it wasn't an accident? Have they arrested Nate yet?"

Cassandra didn't want to get into this with her. She tried to keep her voice neutral while explaining, "Seems like they are still investigating. The tool used on the sword was in Nate's bag, but he swears he didn't use it or put it there. Actually, now they are looking at Shannon Bryant. The college is trying to fire him."

Rhonda sniffled. "But it wasn't his fault! Nate's sword was broken and he's the one who hurt my son."

At a loss for the right words to say, the most authentic thing Cassandra could come up with was, "I'm so sorry this is happening."

After a few more moments of cuddling Murphy and an awkward hug goodbye, they parted ways, Cassandra feeling lower than ever since arriving in Nebraska.

Cassandra drummed her fingernails on the desk as she pulled up Nate Parker's student account, ignoring Gregory's warning the previous day about staying out of student financial records. She scrolled through the screens, noting the 3.3 GPA, Dean's List honors, and an impeccable record of tuition payments all in full and on time.

Leaning back in her chair, she saw Murphy curled up in a white ball of fluff, lightly snoring on his bed in the corner. Clearly, Nate had financial assistance from his family to pay for school. Devon had hinted at their wealth when they'd visited her office together. And there seemed to be no clues here about his character or their roommate problems.

When she switched to Sam Soukup's records, the GPA, late fees he had accrued, and that Carson Future Leaders scholarship were stark differences. She quickly scanned the other names to see if anyone else had been awarded the same scholarship, but it seemed to be a one-time thing.

Frowning, she picked up the phone and dialed the number for the bank listed on the screen. After speaking with a representative, Cassandra was transferred to the manager. A few swift verification questions later and Cassandra discovered something startling. The scholarship account belonged to none other than Dr. Bob Gregory, the college Interim President himself.

Cassandra asked the bank manager, "Does this account fund other students or expenses at Morton College?"

"No, just the one," Cassandra heard tapping on a keyboard for several moments before the manager answered. "Monthly payments. The account was opened nearly three years ago."

Cassandra hung up the phone, her mind calculating. Coincidentally, that was around the same time Sam Soukup would have been a freshman entering Morton. Suddenly Sam's accidental death seemed more sinister. Why was the college president awarding this scholarship to only one student?

More troubling was the realization that Gregory hadn't chosen Sam randomly – he'd been targeting him all along! Something bigger was going on here and Cassandra wasn't going to let it go. Even if that meant going up against an icon like Gregory and sacrificing her career in the process. She'd face the consequences later, right now she was focused on uncovering the truth.

Even though Morton College employed a coven of accountants and computer wizards, Cassandra knew exactly who to call – Andy Summers, the head of campus security.

If she was incorrect in her suspicions about the Interim President, Andy would be more persuasive in convincing her not to jump headfirst into the career suicide abyss.

Accusing Gregory of embezzlement or conspiracy was a delicate matter, one that required enough proof to topple a mountain.

Soon her office door swung open and in came Andy and his former stray pup Buckley, a floppy-eared, orange mutt who outweighed Murphy by almost twenty pounds. Remembering each other from their obedience school days, Murphy and Buckley were quick to show each other a little love by sniffing each other's privates.

Luckily as humans, all Andy said was "Hey, what's up? It sounded urgent."

Cassandra shot a quick look at the students in the outer office before lowering her voice. "Can you shut the door?" she asked.

She pushed the bank statement she'd printed into Andy's hands and explained how this account was unique to the other scholarships in their system. "This doesn't look right. Gregory has been carrying out some shady transactions with this account."

"It doesn't make any sense. Why would he do this?" Andy asked, confusion washing over his face.

Cassandra shrugged. "Your guess is as good as mine. But I think we need to move before he has a chance to cover it up. None of Sam's roommates or his mother Rhonda let on that Sam knew that there was anything unusual about this scholarship. Gregory must have kept it secret for a reason."

Andy said, "What else do you have? This isn't the only strange thing going on in this town."

"No kidding, everyone seems to be keeping secrets. Except my neighbor Mrs. Gill. She's an over-sharer." Cassandra said with a smirk. "I asked Rhonda Soukup if she thought Sam had gambling debts or a drug problem, but she was a bit vague on the day to day details of Sam's life. This scholarship might be totally above board, but with Sam's death and Shannon Bryant's job on the line, we have to dig deeper."

"Gregory does seem to have it out for Shannon," Andy agreed. "You don't really believe they'd fire him just for the one mistake at the play? He's got tenure."

Cassandra wanted to keep Shannon's private life quiet if at all possible, even though Andy wasn't likely to spread rumors about him. If the Human Resources department had evidence that Bryant had lied during his application process, or if the student misconduct incident he'd shared with her was viewed more seriously, he could very well lose his job for cause.

She refocused on the reason she'd asked for Andy's help. "We need to confront Gregory about the scholarship account. Maybe something more is going on here than we're aware of. I called Gregory's assistant but the earliest we could get an appointment with him is later this afternoon."

Chapter Twenty-Three

W HEN THEY ARRIVED FOR the meeting with Dr. Gregory, Cassandra's office had closed for the day, and she hefted her tote bag, coat, and Murphy on his leash so she could head straight home after the meeting.

Cassandra cleared her throat and spoke firmly. "Dr. Gregory, thank you for seeing us on such short notice. We have some questions about a scholarship account that was opened in your name three years ago. We believe it was used to fund a student at Morton College, and we need some answers." She paused and pointed to the security director. "You know Andy Summers from campus security. I thought it was best to have him here."

Gregory's gray brows met over his slender nose, and he looked between the two of them. "Listen, I don't need to answer to you. Anyway, I don't even know what scholarship account you're talking about." His condescending tone grated on Cassandra's nerves. "I'll not have you questioning my authority. Before the board appointed me interim president, I spent thirty years as head of Financial Aid and the Business Office. Isn't your degree in teaching? Like I told you the other day, you should stick to lesson plans and coloring pages and stop meddling in things you don't understand."

Cassandra was horrified by his audacity. Other students struggled financially each semester due lack of access to scholarships, and here Gregory was playing God with his little pot of money.

She quietly laid out the bank statements showing the income and payments from Gregory's personal bank account. "This is the account from the bank downtown," she said. "We need to know why it was opened, what it was used for, and why you kept it secret."

"You had no authorization to view these. I told you to stay in your lane or suffer the consequences, young lady!"

Cassandra rose to her towering height of five-foot-five, thankful she'd chosen three-inch heels that morning. Her nostrils flared as her voice remained calm. "The deposits and payments from Morton College are within my purview as an administrator. When I spoke with the bank manager about our concern that someone might be embezzling funds, she shared these statements with me." Her eyes settled on Andy Summers who was wearing his Morton College security uniform. "You might want to think more carefully about your next statement, sir," she said. "Mr. Summers will be including it word for word in his formal report."

Gregory opened and closed his mouth like a fish, saliva bubbling in the corners. He cleared his throat. "My apologies, I was out of line. He looked at Andy who had been watching quietly until now and said, "I sent money to Sam Soukup through the college accounts, but it wasn't for any illegal purpose."

He nervously adjusted his glasses and began to explain the situation. Bob Soukup had asked him for a favor – to help support his grandson with college tuition payments. Gregory had agreed because he knew the relationship between Soukup and his daughter had been strained for years. He wanted to make sure Sam had the chance to pursue a higher education after everything that had happened. As he finished his explanation, he ran trembling hands through his thinning hair. He explained that he hadn't realized how complicated it would be to keep it hidden from the board and other administrators at Morton College. He paused, looking between Cassandra and Andy.

Cassandra's eyes narrowed with understanding, and she let out a long sigh. "You've been lying for almost three years and paying this student through the Morton College financial aid system. You're finished as President."

Gregory's anger erupted like a volcano. "You can't be serious!" he bellowed, although his rage quickly subsided when he noticed Murphy standing in front of Cassandra, teeth bared in a snarling growl. Gregory blinked in disbelief and took a few steps back, calming himself.

Cassandra couldn't help but smile at this tiny sign of love from the pup. She knew she had made the right decision in adopting Murphy three months prior at the same time Andy had rescued his dog. Murphy had been aloof to her commands and touches. Not to mention the obedience classes at the animal hospital were only mildly effective. But today he came to her aid trying to protect her from the president's anger.

Cassandra felt a rush of adrenaline as she stared at President Gregory, unable to believe what she was hearing. Whatever secret financial arrangement he had worked out with Bob Soukup must have been important enough for Gregory to risk everything for it.

She clenched her fists and stepped forward, her voice steady and controlled. "President Gregory," she said firmly but calmly. "I understand you are doing what you think is right for Morton College, but it goes against all our rules and policies." She paused and shifted her gaze toward Andy who nodded in agreement then back toward President Gregory. "We have no choice but to bring this information to the Board of Directors."

President Gregory's shoulders slumped forward in resignation as he let out a heavy sigh. He looked at them with pleading eyes, his voice soft and desperate. "Please," he said. "Do not make this matter public knowledge yet. I just need a little more time ..." His words hung in the air, as if expecting them to understand his unspoken plea.

Cassandra knew President Gregory needed a way out of this mess without destroying his career, and she was determined to give him one.

"How much time do you need, sir?" Her consideration was way more than he'd ever given anyone else.

They waited in silence while the large grandfather clock on the fireplace mantel loudly ticked off the seconds. President Gregory's expression shifted from shock to defeat. He finally seemed to grasp that brusquely shoving this aside wasn't going to work. He changed tactics.

Pasting an uncomfortable smile on his face, he said, "Just a few more days to put some things in order."

Cassandra picked up Murphy's leash and her coat, ready to leave the office, when Andy caught her eye and mouthed a word to her.

She nodded and turned back to President Gregory. "Okay, but first we need you to do one thing."

Cassandra and Andy entered the conference room, carrying the evidence they had gathered on Dr. Gregory's financial arrangement with Bob Soukup. They were eager to present their findings to Chairman Alan Hershey.

As they took their seats at the long table, Cassandra and Andy exchanged nervous glances. They knew Hershey was a nice guy whose full head of hair was never out of place, but they were unsure how he would react to their news.

But before they could even begin their presentation, Mr. Hershey looked from Cassandra to Andy expectantly, "So, what do you two have for me?"

Andy cleared his throat and began, "We believe we have evidence that Dr. Gregory has been involved in a secret financial arrangement with Bob Soukup. The details of their scheme are still unclear, but based on our investigation, it appears that Dr. Gregory was working with Mr. Soukup to fund his personal projects."

Chairman Hershey leaned back in his chair and steepled his fingers together as he digested the information they had presented. After a few moments of silence, he said slowly, "This is very serious indeed. I need to take some time to think about this matter before I decide how we should proceed. Isn't the memorial service for Mr. Soukup's grandson scheduled for tomorrow morning? Let's press pause on our investigation for now," he said, his tone measured and calm. "Out of respect for the Soukup family and friends."

Cassandra felt her heart sink and feared they had wasted their efforts in gathering evidence against Dr. Gregory when the Chairman added, "However, I must commend you both for your hard work and dedication to uncovering this information. It's clear that you both care deeply about Morton College."

Cassandra was taken aback. She had expected some resistance, but not anticipated such a sudden halt to their momentum. "Excuse me?" Cassandra tried to keep the frustration out of her voice. "We're talking about possibly illegal transactions."

Hershey looked directly at her. "I understand your concerns, but we need to be careful here. Bob Soukup is a valuable member of this community, and we don't want to upset him unnecessarily."

The tension in the room was palpable as Hershey looked from Cassandra to Andy, silently asking them to concur. She was already at odds with Gregory, and getting on Hershey's wrong side wasn't a politically astute move, either.

As Andy nodded, Chairman Hershey took a deep breath and stood up from the table. "Very well," he said. "Let's put this matter on hold for now. I'm sure you both have other important things to take care of today."

Cassandra felt a wave of frustration surge through her as the chairman walked out of the room. She knew Soukup's wealth and influence had a tight grip on the town, but she couldn't help feeling that Hershey's motives were more about self-preservation and taking the easy way out than anything else.

Deflated, she clutched the file folder to her chest and silently walked alongside Andy all the way down the hallway to her office.

As soon as her office door closed behind them, she blurted, "Fine! Hershey doesn't want us poking into whatever Gregory and Soukup have going on. I get that. But we have no time to waste if we're going to help Shannon Bryant keep his job."

"There is one angle that might help," Andy said. "There were so many people who had the opportunity to tamper with props. It seems flimsy that Shannon would have known differently if he'd done the final checks that night."

"I saw that backstage area during warm ups and it seemed like kids were coming and going pretty freely right up until curtain time." Cassandra said, "That detail might help prove Shannon's innocence, but I dislike the idea of deflecting blame away from one innocent person by pointing at someone else without real proof first."

"I can run a background check on Shannon and find out anything in his past they can use against him," said Andy.

"You can try, but he already told me about a past incident that got him into trouble. There was a situation with a graduate student who eventually became became his wife. I want to avoid digging up more gossip about him, right? Some of his students work in my office," Cassandra added. "They'd do anything to support him. In fact, when they get wind of his suspension, they'll probably start a revolt. Then Gregory's financial problems will seem like small potatoes compared to firing one of the most popular tenured professors on campus."

Cassandra sat down at her desk, feeling a surge of determination. They might not be able to take down Gregory and Soukup directly, but they could certainly find a way to help Shannon. They just had to be clever about it.

Chapter Twenty-Four

CASSANDRA POPPED INTO THE bathroom of the Arts Center, checking her eye makeup for smudges. The hour-long memorial service for Sam Soukup had just let out, and a few tears had rolled down her cheeks as she said her final goodbye. The chapel bells tolled, their echoes coming in waves across campus.

The students from Simon Harris's Death 101 class had done an amazing job using information they'd learned from their assignments, handling every aspect of the service with care and grace. A few of them had even gone with his mom Rhonda to choose a simple urn for his ashes. From selecting the somber yet uplifting music to moving Bible passages, they had walked the delicate balance of honoring Sam's life.

She had watched in awe as Devon McKenzie delivered a heartfelt eulogy, his voice unwavering despite the emotion evident in his eyes. Cassandra felt a lump in her throat as she realized that, even though he had been upset with Sam for months, Devon was here today to honor him in front of the hundred-plus mourners. The service had been personal and touching but also included some funny stories about things Sam had done as a child and student. When Devon stepped away from the podium, Rhonda Soukup walked over to him and gave him a big hug.

As the service drew to a close, Simon Harris stepped into the white glow of the stage lights, and the theatre was filled with a hush of anticipation among the crowd paying their respects. He announced that the cast and crew would be performing the play again in its entirety in memory of Sam, with proceeds from the ticket sales going toward a special scholarship fund to be established in his name for the following year.

Meg O'Brien emerged from a bathroom stall, adjusting her black interpreter's outfit, and washed her hands. "College kids," she muttered under her breath. "Partying and Netflix binges one minute, then acting all thoughtful and mature the next. You'd think they'd make up their minds already."

"I don't know how you do it," Cassandra said, joining her. "I'd be a blubbering mess if I had to be on stage like you, in front of all those people, interpreting those words and not letting emotions get the better of me."

"I'm heartless," Meg joked with a smirk. "No, really. I just get so focused on doing my linguistic gymnastics that I don't allow the words to sink into my body. Easier said than done, though, I know."

When Cassandra opened the bathroom door, a scene of chaos filled the lobby. Shannon Bryant, recently suspended, had attracted a crowd of students. Handshakes were exchanged and a vigorous sign language conversation began.

Chairman Hershey stood nearby, nervously eyeing the students. He shifted left and right, trying to find a way to wiggle through the crowd and escape but unable to move too far away without attracting attention.

But he was not fast enough.

"You can't fire Dr. Bryant," a student called out, loud enough for Cassandra to hear. Hershey's eyes widened and he took a giant step back, looking for a better exit route.

"He's one of the best professors I've ever had," announced a tall student, who seemed to tower over everyone else in the group. "You're on the board of directors, right? You can overrule them, can't you?"

Hershey blushed as if he was caught red-handed. He was in the hot seat now and had nowhere to hide. An angry crowd had him surrounded with no way out.

"Umm, this really isn't the best time or place to have this discussion," Hershey stammered. "Dr. Bryant is only suspended currently, and a final decision will be made by administration."

The student chatter quieted as all eyes fell on Mr. Hershey and Shannon. Meg stepped into the center of the circle and when Shannon Bryant looked her way, she began interpreting what everyone was saying.

Shannon Bryant's face flushed as he realized they were talking about him. He threw up his hands as if he were a police officer stopping traffic. He signed and Meg spoke in English, *Thank you all for your support. I really appreciate what you're trying to do. If you want to help me, send emails to President Gregory and the board.* Shannon motioned to the Chairman. *For now, let's just let Mr. Hershey pass through the lobby, okay? We're all upset about the way things have turned out. The best thing you can do right now is go home and do something kind.*

Hershey, with a curt bob of his still perfectly quaffed head, navigated the throng of people as if they were an obstacle course. He cast one last glance over his shoulder and glided out the door without saying a word.

Next to Cassandra, Cinda watched the whole incident unfold and drawled, "Well, ain't he just as useful as a screen door on a submarine?"

Cassandra huffed a quiet laugh. "That's one way to put it." But the humor barely registered, because her mind was already on what she needed to do next.

Shannon remained a few moments before bidding them goodbye, his glasses glinting off the overhead light as he bowed out.

"Hey, do you have to hurry off, too?" Cassandra asked Cinda. "I'd like you and Meg to come with me for a few minutes."

Soon Cassandra led Cinda and Meg to the campus chapel garden. A soft burble of water cascaded from the fountain ahead, where they found a bench with pretty flowers all around it.

"This is the place," Cassandra said with a raspy voice. "I've been talking to some of the kids from the Death 101 class," Cassandra said, pulling a sheet of stationery from her blazer pocket. "They were given an assignment to write a goodbye letter to someone they had lost. I thought it might help me, too."

Meg squeezed her arm gently. "Take your time, Cass, it's going to be alright."

Cassandra's hands trembled as she read it aloud.

"To my dearest Paul,

It's been a whole six years since I last saw you and your adorable dimples. But when I look at photos of you, I'm still swooning like the first day we met.

I miss you more than chocolate cake on my cheat day, and it hurts me to know that we never got to live as a married couple or bring our babies into this world. You would have had the cutest sons. My head knows I must move on, but my heart is too stubborn!

I wish I had known how serious your virus was and maybe I would not be writing this letter. But wishes aren't plans, and dreams don't always come true, so here I am just saying thank you for everything you brought into my life.

Know that I will always cherish our memories and hold dear the lessons you taught me. Wherever you are now, I hope you're smiling down on me with love. And I hope you're proud of the person I've become.

Thinking of you with love and longing.

Yours forever, Cassandra."

She tucked the paper back into her pocket. Meg hugged her hard, and Cinda patted her shoulder. "He was lucky to have someone like you love him."

"I always will." Cassandra nodded. They all wiped tears from under their eyes for a few moments.

"Let's grab something to eat," Cassandra said, a hint of cheer in her soggy voice. "Shedding emotional baggage makes me hungry!"

Meg shook her head. "Rain check? I'd love to, but I have to get to Biology class soon."

"Me too," Cinda said, "I have a lunch date with a salad at my desk while I catch up on everything I missed this morning."

Meg and Cinda shot Cassandra a quick nod, then darted off toward the admin building as if free ice cream were waiting for them inside.

Talk about suspicious.

"Hey, I've been looking for you." Fischer's voice close behind her made her jump and a little eep noise escaped as she spun around to face him. He was dressed up in gray golf pants and a polo shirt with a Morton College quarter zip fleece and smelled woodsy like a forest.

No wonder Meg and Cinda had scurried off without warning, they must have seen him lurking in the background.

She cleared her throat, "You found me." It would have been nice if she'd come up with something more interesting to say than that—something witty or dramatic—but no such luck.

"No worries, I have sisters," Fischer joked. "I can recognize an intense girl moment when I see one."

Cassandra hesitated, debating whether or not to tell him about the letter she wrote. But what the heck? She decided to be bold and tell him the truth.

"Yeah, ...we were doing a sort of goodbye ritual." She glanced down at her navy dress pumps, which had a scuff on the outside of the right shoe. "I wrote a goodbye letter to Paul. Like the kids in the Death 101 class wrote for one of their homework assignments. It seemed like a good way to get closure, so I thought I'd try."

When he didn't say anything right away, she raised her eyes to meet his intense blue gaze. "Did it help?" He asked, "With the closure, I mean."

"Maybe ..." Inhaling a big breath, she examined her feelings. No tightness in her lungs. Dry eyes. Stomach normal. Heart ...yeesh, his eyes were as clear as the ocean near Oahu's North Shore. If she stared at those eyes too long, she might lose herself in them. "I feel a lightness," her fingers rested over her heart, "here."

"That's encouraging news." His face slowly inched closer to hers and her heart skipped a beat.

Then, she thought of what Terrance Zimmerman had said about seeing Fischer and Fran Morrison together. She lightly put her palm on his chest and halted his progress. "Hang on. What was the story with you and Fran Morrison at the Field House?"

"What?" He backed up, his fists moving to his hips, "the Field House—"

"No sidestepping this," she warned. "I want the truth. I know you met with her, but as a search committee member, you had to know it goes against protocol."

He took hold of her arms, squeezing gently in a reassuring way. "We didn't talk about the president's job. C'mon, you've known me for what, seven months now? Don't you trust me yet?"

"I was right. You did know Fran before!" Her stomach cramped into a fist sized ball. "Why did you keep it secret from the committee? It's something to do with Iraq, isn't it?"

"Did you check up on us? Did you call around about it?"

The ball in her stomach grew. "No, just my instincts. You were acting weird around her, and I could tell you knew each other."

Before her thoughts spiraled too far out of control, he said firmly, "Yes, we do know each other from Iraq. No, I can't tell you more, because it has nothing to do with Morton. I'm asking you to trust me."

She made herself take in another deep breath. The last time she had completely put her faith in a man, he had—

Gently Fischer pulled her into a hug. "I won't leave unless you want me to," he whispered in her ear. "I'm in love with you."

She let his warmth settle around her, then leaned back to look into his face, "I don't know if I—"

"You don't have to say it back. I just want you to know I'm for real."

His eyes were intense, but there was an undeniable kindness behind them that seemed too hard for her to resist any longer. She raised up onto her tiptoes and pressed her lips against his. She still wanted answers, but for now, she would trust her heart.

Chapter Twenty-Five

WEDGED INTO ONE OF three 1950s-style diner booths on the gas station side of the Gas and Sweets, Cassandra eyed the small laminated menu discolored by what she hoped was an old ketchup stain. From its wood paneling, to the neon beer signs, and the red swivel-stool seats by the counter, everything was covered in a thin layer of grime. Next to her, Andy Summers rested comfortably with one arm propped on the back of the bench behind her shoulder.

Across the table, Chairman Hershey looked out of place in his suit and preppy button-down shirt that would have fit in better at the country club.

Seated at the table directly behind them, a laughing group of grizzled farmers who looked old enough to be retired nursed their coffees and made plans to meet later that afternoon for cards at the American Legion Hall.

Cassandra had warned her table mates that this was a horrible idea, but here they were, camped out in their little booth, waiting for Bob Soukup to check a customer out at the register, so they could get his attention.

Hershey and Andy had played it cool, but she was too embarrassed to even look Bob Soukup in the face. She didn't want to know what was going on in the kitchen of this health code violation in the making. Still, they had a mission, and it was time to get it done.

As the fates would have it, the farmers left the same time as the customer. The store's decibel level dropped to a much more comfortable level, and Mr. Soukup sat next to Hershey.

"Alan, good to see you. Thanks again for coming to my grandson's memorial yesterday. Means a lot to the family that the college was represented. Now what brings you here today? Looking for a donation for a new building?"

Alan Hershey cleared his throat. "Actually, Bob, we have some questions about the private scholarship you funded for Sam through Morton's Financial Aid office."

Soukup had the grace to look ashamed. "I guess Gregory told you about it, huh?" He sighed, "Him and his big mouth. Not much of a friend, is he?"

Hershey shook his head. "What were you two thinking? What you've done was illegal as all get out. If you wanted to help with your grandson's education, why didn't you just write him a check?"

"I suppose I wanted to make amends," he said slowly. "You wouldn't understand."

"Convince me," Hershey said with a wave of his hand.

Soukup looked through the sliding glass doors into the bakery side of the Gas and Sweets where his daughter Rhonda was boxing up items for a short line of customers.

"She wouldn't have it. Wanted to take care of her son on her own. Couldn't believe when they moved back here three years ago and she agreed to open her bakery in my building. Too bad her mama wasn't around to see that day..." Soukup's voice tapered off with his attention for a few moments while he seemed to flash back to a happier time. "I know money doesn't buy love or forgiveness, but it's all I had left to give and it seemed like the best way to help."

Cassandra had never seen the old man be so talkative before, she thought with bemusement. He'd been a bear in all the meetings she attended on campus.

"I hadn't seen Sam for years after they moved away and she split from his daddy," Soukup went on. "Told me I was bad news and not to go near them. Said I was a cutthroat businessman, and it wasn't healthy for her or the boy to spend time around someone like me."

That's exactly what Cassandra had heard since Day One on the job at Morton. While no one had ever come right out and accused him, everyone just assumed he was connected with some shady characters.

Frankly, she was mystified that the college even wanted him on their board of directors, but she guessed it had more to do with his large financial donations and less to do with his friendly personality.

Andy said, "If the board presses charges against President Gregory and you, it will cost his job. You both might end up in court."

"Isn't it bad enough my grandson is gone?" Soukup waved a hand vaguely like he could wipe away his transgressions. "We'll shut everything down at the bank. No one needs to know about it now."

But I know, thought Cassandra. Her face betrayed her feelings when she locked eyes with Soukup.

"I know what you're thinking," Soukup sneered. He jutted his chin toward Rhonda's shop. "Just like her. You think the crusty old man is too cold-hearted to be worth your time. Well let me tell you something." Soukup was getting riled up, just like Cassandra was used to seeing at business meetings. "I've got news for the both of you. Sam didn't think I was too cold-hearted. His mother doesn't know this, but he started coming around here to see me on her days off. We were just starting to get closer and I was gonna teach him so many things if only we had more time."

Soukup's face twisted in pain, and he looked away, collecting himself.

Cassandra felt awful for coming here the day after Sam's memorial and stirring up emotions that were already raw.

Rhonda suddenly materialized several feet from their table. Apparently, she'd come through the kitchen. Dark circles bordered her eyes like she'd been awake for days. Her ponytail was loose and greasy, and truly she looked slightly unhinged. Rhonda dropped a blue backpack at her feet, a bundle of envelopes clutched tightly in her hand.

Andy perked up, and Hershey frowned.

Rhonda didn't even notice them as she huffed through chapped lips, "The kids who cleaned out Sam's things brought these over last night. It was enlightening." If it were possible, deadly lasers would've shot out of her eyes toward her father. "I can't believe you had the gall to go behind my back." She slammed the mail down and pointed an accusing finger. "Your letters were in his room, Dad. You were giving him money? Telling him to keep it a secret from me?"

"Just a few dollars here and there. I swear he never knew about the tuition, honey. He thought it was a legit scholarship." Soukup's face turned tomato red. "I was just trying to help. You've never been able to take care of yourself, Rhonda. I didn't want Sam to end up ...like you."

"Like me? You mean independent? Capable? You don't get to talk to me about taking care of myself. You didn't earn the right to give him advice."

The tension in the room was stifling, and Cassandra felt like she was intruding on a private family matter. She made eye contact with Andy, and they silently agreed that it was time to leave.

But Rhonda was on a tear. She grabbed one of the letters and unfolded the page. "Get this. Just what every twenty-year-old needs to hear." She read from the paper in a deep voice mimicking her father's. "'Remember, Sam, the world is a competitive place. If you want to succeed, you have to be willing to do whatever it takes. Don't let anyone stand in your way, and don't be afraid to use every tool at your disposal.'"

Rhonda tossed that one on the table and grabbed another. "'Sam, you're a born leader. You have a natural charisma that draws people to you. But sometimes, you have to be willing to step on a few toes to get what you want. Don't be afraid to make enemies if it means achieving your goals.'"

Hershey looked confused, Andy looked concerned, and Cassandra was speechless.

"You sound more like the Godfather instead of the grandfather!" Rhonda scoffed. "What Sam did to Nate at *The Three Musketeers?* That's totally on you, Dad."

Soukup's eyes widened. "What are you talking about?"

"You used your money and tried to control him. He was too proud to ask me for help saving for his backpacking trip because he knew I'd say no. When Sam complained to me about Nate having such an easy life, I told him to work harder. You took advantage of a vulnerable boy and encouraged him to cross the line."

Even though Rhonda and her father shared a last name and a building, it seemed they hadn't communicated directly like this in years.

Cassandra desperately wished she could say something to stop this train wreck from happening. She'd learned that sometimes people just have to vent, then you pick up the pieces after it's over.

Rhonda reached inside the blue backpack and pulled out a flannel button-down shirt. "At first, I thought it was glitter. See?" She shoved the cloth under her father's nose, then held it out for the rest to see. "It's all over the shirt and little pieces are in the backpack too. But it's not glitter. It looks like metal shavings. Like the kind of dusty pieces that would cover your clothes if you had used a file to shave off parts of your roommate's sword."

It took several heartbeats for the implications of Rhonda's revelation to sink in, like struggling to see through murky water. Sam was the one who had tampered with Nate's sword. Cassandra's jaw dropped.

"Congratulations, Dad," said Rhonda. "Sam took your advice to use any *tool* at his disposal, hoping to make Nate look like a fool in front of the entire town. And instead, my son is gone."

So, Sam's intention was to get back at his roommate using a childish prank. Instead Sam's bad judgment caused his own death from the broken hilt? He made a permanent fix to a temporary problem. Cassandra, Andy, and Alan Hershey exchanged horrified glances. The tragedy of it all was almost too much to bear.

Soukup's face turned ashen. "You have no physical proof."

Rhonda handed the shirt to Andy. "You can test it, right? Compare the metals?"

Andy examined the cloth for several moments and nodded. "Yes ma'am. I'll take care of it." He touched the letters. "Can I borrow these too? I can ask around and see if there are more connections or evidence."

But Cassandra suspected the testing would be simply a formality. Rhonda had known something was wrong with her son, but hadn't discovered the seriousness of the situation until it was too late.

Rhonda handed the letters to Andy and stared hard at Soukup. "My son is dead. Because of your stupidity."

Unable to meet his daughter's accusing gaze, he hung his head. "No—no! I—I didn't mean for that to happen."

"I believe you. Yet, here we are." With that, she turned on her heel and left, the sound of the bell ringing over the door the final punctuation to her declaration.

After a moment of stunned silence, Soukup hefted himself off the bench and wandered to the back of the store.

Cassandra felt a pang of sympathy for Soukup. It was obvious he had loved his grandson and was genuinely sorry. But no matter how she looked at it, his meddling and underhanded tactics had set this tragedy in motion.

Chapter Twenty-Six

AT THE APPOINTED TIME, Cassandra, Andy Summers, and Alan Hershey met with Bob Gregory at his office. The heavy curtains were wide open, flooding the room with light, a stark contrast to the tense atmosphere as they took their seats.

Dr. Gregory's tall figure dwarfed the leather executive chair, and he held his head high, "What can I do for you today?"

"So, it looks like you've been playing fast and loose with the budget." Alan Hershey was not one to mince words. "You know why we're here. Bob Soukup's grandson Sam was granted a secret scholarship through your office. What are you going to do to remedy that?"

Gregory's eyes narrowed at Cassandra. She'd promised him time, but apparently two days wasn't what he'd had in mind.

"I already told her. The president serves at the pleasure of the Board of Directors. It wasn't my place to question the orders of a board member like Bob Soukup." He shifted in his chair, beads of sweat forming on his forehead. "After all, what damage could really come from helping out one student with tuition payments?"

Hershey continued, "In addition to the scholarship, where else have you rearranged the budget allocations? The board has made numerous tough choices over the past 18 months based on your advice and financial projections. I'm guessing you've fudged the money picture to make it appear the situation is more critical than it is, like with the theater department. I've no faith in your trustworthiness and have ordered a complete audit."

Hershey paused, letting his words sink in. "You must resign from your position or face the consequences," he concluded.

At first, Gregory refused. "Absolutely not," he said firmly. "I've done nothing wrong, and I won't be bullied into anything."

Hershey listened to Dr. Gregory's arguments, but his expression remained unyielding. "If you do not resign," he said, "Morton will pursue legal action and will bring the issue to the media."

Cassandra heard the clock ticking, counting off the remaining seconds of Gregory's presidency. A fly on the windowsill buzzed and crawled. Hershey and Gregory stared each other down.

Dr. Gregory was cornered, but he wasn't going to give in that easily. They seemed to be at an impasse.

Cassandra could see an opportunity in this moment, and she stepped in. "Here's a proposal," she said with more confidence than she actually felt. "If you agree to reverse the funding cuts to the theater department and drop the case against Dr. Bryant with no fanfare, Mr. Hershey will sign off on your retirement papers without going public with any detailed reasons for your departure. It would show everyone that Morton College puts their students first. This way we can undo some of the damage," she went on, "and it might redeem the school's reputation."

After a few moments of thought, Dr. Gregory yielded with a giant sigh, agreeing to fulfill their requests and promising to sign papers reversing both decisions immediately.

Once they were out of his office, Cassandra did an exuberant cha cha slide down the hallway while Hershey praised them for a job well done before departing.

Back in her office with Andy, Cassandra tossed out high fives like candy at the Lei Day parade. Rachel and Lance were working the reception area and gave them confused looks, but Cassandra just signed, *It's a good day*, before sailing into her office and closing the door.

"That was amazing!" Cassandra exclaimed. "We pulled off our mission without any major drama or conflict, and Shannon's personal life stays out of the public headlines. His ex-wife and daughter won't have to deal with nosy police inquiries or prying school investigations. I can't believe we managed to juggle all those different interests," she said in amazement.

"We are ninja negotiators," said Andy. "Did you see Gregory's face when you told him your plan? I thought he was going to choke on his own tongue."

Cassandra smiled proudly, as she topped off her coffee cup. "Forget Queen of Doom. My new title is Empress of Diplomacy."

Cassandra felt a shiver of anticipation as she fidgeted in her seat at the Performing Arts Center, sandwiched between Cinda, her husband Jacob, and Fischer. Despite having to recast a role in *The Three Musketeers* after the chaotic debut performance the week before, there was an air of anticipation as the actors took to the stage.

Cassandra's mind strayed to her parents who had been sitting here with her last time and she felt an ache of missing them, remembering the quality time they had spent together during their visit. If she were totally honest, she also missed her mom's cooking.

To her right, Cassandra saw Terrance Zimmerman sitting with a young boy. At first, she thought it was one of his children, but as she studied them, she recognized Michael, the shoplifting boy from the gas station convenience store. Frowning, she asked Cinda, "Is that boy related to Terrance? Do you know him?"

"No, that's his Buddy Match." Cinda said, "Terrance mentors him through a cool local school program."

Cassandra made a mental note to check into the Buddy Match program more later. It sounded like a neat opportunity for both the kids and adult mentors.

Rhonda quietly sat with Margie Gallagher ahead of Cassandra, shoulders tense, radiating a silent need for solitude that Cassandra could respect. She couldn't have gone out in public only a week after Paul's death. But maybe Rhonda didn't want to miss the special tributes they'd do in Sam's memory. To the far left on stage, a feathered hat, yellow rose, and pistol rested on a stool. Cassandra's heart ached for her friend.

Nate's entrance with the other musketeers made all eyes turn eagerly towards the stage, and soon Cassandra was hooked by the energy of the cast and promise of a passionate performance ahead.

The crowd buzzed with excitement as D'Artagnan began his quest to become one of the legendary musketeer guards of King Louis III. Though some might have loved the sword fighting, Cassandra was there for the lavish costumes and romantic drama. The acting and production were really well done, especially considering how they had pulled in students and community members to round out the cast and crew.

During intermission, Fischer leaned over to Cassandra and Cinda, "I heard that Hershey made them swap out the stage prop swords for wooden versions this time. He wasn't taking any chances."

"I'm okay with it," said Cassandra. "Too much realism would spike my anxiety level right now."

"Bless your heart," Cinda said, "you're tougher than a two-dollar steak. You got this!" She squeezed Cassandra's arm.

Cassandra frowned, wondering exactly how tough a two-dollar steak was, until she remembered it was just one of Cinda's Southern sayings.

The second act began with a scene where D'Artagnan meets the beautiful Constance Bonacieux, a lady-in-waiting to Queen Anne, who in turn is being pursued by the evil Cardinal Richelieu. When it was time for the sword fight scene, there was an eerie hush in the audience. Nate stepped out from the wings with the other musketeers and bandits, putting on an impressive show of stage combat as if he'd been doing it for years instead of weeks.

The audience roared with approval when the curtains dropped, and the students took their bows. Cassandra spotted Sela Roberts among the cast as one of D'Artagnan's admirers. With her full stage makeup and costume, she was even more beautiful than usual.

As Nate came out for his solo bow, his face reddened as a wave of whoops and catcalls filled the theater. As first, he seemed stunned by the audience's reaction, then he covered his face with his hands and rushed offstage. She and Cinda would check on him after the play. This must have been so hard.

Simon Harris couldn't resist stealing the show next, waving proudly like he'd won an Oscar. But President Gregory had one more surprise in his pocket, swooping in and adjusting the mic dramatically. "Ladies and gentlemen, thank you for attending this special show. I have one more announcement to make."

Cassandra held her breath.

She and Andy had forced him to go along with the show and the theater department budget, but neither of them had expected him to speak. If Gregory went rogue, the only way to stop him would be by running up onto stage and yanking the microphone before he could embarrass them all.

"It's my pleasure to announce that the Sam Soukup Memorial Scholarship will fully fund one student next academic year and continue to accept donations from the community for years to come." Gregory adjusted his tie and cleared his throat. "As for me, I bid you all adieu. I have officially resigned my position at Morton College. It's time for me to drive around in my RV and take some time off. The new president will be announced soon." He made a small formal bow and exited stage right.

The audience was baffled for a moment about what the appropriate response was to such an announcement. But they soon recovered enough to give a quiet golf clap to the now empty stage.

"Controlling the narrative," Cassandra murmured.

Cinda did several loud claps. "Good riddance," she cheered.

Cassandra met Fischer's eyes and they both burst into laughter.

Chapter Twenty–Seven

Interim President Gregory's personal belongings hadn't even been removed from his suite in the admin building before the search committee convened for its final task in the process of confirming his replacement. Cassandra took her seat at the boardroom table and sipped an iced Kona coffee latte from her travel mug.

When Terrance Zimmerman spotted her, he sank into the chair next to hers so he could speak quietly. "I contacted the accreditation agency's liaison to tell them no charges were being brought by the college or local police regarding the play incident. The agency agreed the college wasn't negligent in the student's death, and said they'd halt their investigation of Morton's string of unfortunate events."

"That's a relief," Cassandra said. "Let's hope our luck is changing."

Terrance resumed his seat at the head of the table so he could lead the meeting, beginning with a moment of silence in honor of Sam Soukup. The sadness in the room was thick, like dense air pressure before a summer storm, but they tried to push it away and focus on business.

"Let's welcome Alan Hershey to the discussion," Terrance said, "representing the board of directors, as Bob Soukup is unable to attend."

Whether his absence was by Soukup's choice or the board's request, Cassandra didn't need to know, but either way it would make the meeting less awkward.

Terrance asked Gia to begin summarizing the pros and cons of each candidate. Halfway down the list for the John Goodman lookalike candidate, Gia said, "He has some traditional viewpoints and appears to relish the customary social engagements that come with the role."

Cassandra winced while she studied the body language of the others around the table. Surely they weren't in favor of that caveman! If you needed someone to tell Dad Jokes and grill you a burger wearing a "King of the Grill" apron during Memorial Day Weekend, he was probably your guy. No way would she entrust a multi-million dollar learning enterprise to that man.

Bob Soukup had supported him, so that should be another strike against him.

When it was Cassandra's turn to offer the pros and cons for hiring Fran Morrison, she only had a few cons—one of them being a prior relationship with her boyfriend, which she couldn't mention in public. On the plus side, she mentioned Fran's fund raising ideas, budgeting experience, and youthful energy.

"It seems clear to me that our best choice is Fran Morrison," Cassandra summarized. "Her interview and presentation gave us all a glimpse into how passionate she is about continuing this college's legacy of excellence and bringing facilities up to par with our peer institutions. I think we can all agree on this point?"

After further discussion, the committee chose Fran Morrison by unanimous vote. Gia said jokingly, "Well then, I guess we'd better adjourn now before anybody changes their mind!"

Mr. Hershey looked relieved that they had finally decided on a new leader for Morton, and he could go back to his normal role as board chairman. Cassandra didn't envy all the extra work he had taken on during the past three months since President Nielson's death.

As everyone stood up and gathered their papers, Terrance said, "I'm so glad we'll have a new leader with expertise and enthusiasm for transforming this college. She's exactly what we need."

Mr. Hershey cleared his throat before saying, "Remember that although this decision is final, it's only one step on our journey towards success. We still need to work together if we want Morton to reach its true potential."

Everyone nodded solemnly in agreement before Gia said, "There's no time like now to get started! Shall we head over to The Home Team to celebrate our work today?"

"I was already planning to meet Andy and Shannon later," Cassandra said. "We're finally getting around to celebrating the acceptance of our telecommunications grant proposal."

"Great! We can watch the end of the basketball game," Fischer said. "My March Madness bracket is dead, but I want to watch anyway."

They agreed to meet in thirty minutes.

Back in her office, Cassandra hooked up Murphy's leash, packed her tote bag for home, and texted Andy.

Cassandra

There's a group going to the bar. You're welcome to invite your girlfriend to join us.

Andy Summers

Yeah, no. Thanks for the thought, but she's no longer in the picture.

Cassandra

Ope. Sorry about that.

Cassandra had recently learned the new Midwestern word *ope* and realized it fit in lots of situations. Kind of like a cross between *oops* and *uh-oh*. With Andy's girlfriend out of the picture, she wondered if he would resume his former crush on her. But quickly, she quashed that thought because she was supposed to be focusing on her future with Fischer.

A few minutes later, Cassandra slumped in her desk chair, feeling a mix of emotions. The initial elation from the search committee decision had worn off, leaving her slightly underwhelmed. As she sat there, a wave of introspection washed over Cassandra, and she chuckled at herself. "You know," she muttered to Murphy, "I've been so serious about my job, treating it like the holy grail of my existence. Maybe it's time to lighten up a bit."

She imagined herself as a *wahine koa,* a woman warrior boss, wearing a cape and carrying a spear to staff meetings. The image brought a genuine laugh bubbling out of her. "Now *that* would shake things up," she mused, "though I might scare off a few colleagues in the process."

Murphy barked in reply, but even though Cassandra studied his chocolate brown eyes, she couldn't guess what he was thinking. "What do you think, Murph'? Have I been wrong to think of Morton as a stepping stone toward something greater?"

But Murphy had already bored of her monologue and laid his head on his front paws waiting for her to take his leash and do something fun. "You might be right. The job isn't just a title or a paycheck. It's part of my identity." She stooped to scratch behind his ears and whisper to him. "You're so smart. I'm glad you have my back."

As this understanding settled within her, Cassandra's thoughts expanded beyond her professional life. She acknowledged that there were other areas in her life that deserved attention. The longings she had tucked away—the desire for a romantic partner, the dream of having a family—had been overshadowed by her single-minded focus on her career. But now, she saw an opportunity to explore those facets of her life as well.

Taking his leash, she turned off the lights and locked the doors behind her. "Maybe it's time to look into those dreams I've kept hidden," Cassandra said, as though Murphy were still listening. "The students are what, only ten years younger than me? I'm still young and anything is possible."

She smiled, feeling the mental weight shift from her new perspective. The daunting task of transforming her dreams into reality didn't discourage her. "What do you say, brah? Let's roll."

Chapter Twenty-Eight

Cassandra dropped Murphy off at her house, and as she stepped into The Home Team, she was hit with a wave of noise and mouthwatering scents. Sizzling bacon, salted peanuts, aged whiskey, and beer mingled in the air, creating an earthy, comforting aroma. The sports bar was buzzing with March Madness games blaring from strategically positioned television screens. Cassandra maneuvered her way through the crowded tables, drawn towards the familiar faces of her coworkers and the lively conversations filled with banter and laughter.

Meg had saved a seat for Cassandra between her and Bryant at the long wooden table, which was already covered in pitchers of beer and bowls of whole peanuts. Terrance Zimmerman, always the attentive one, poured a glass of beer and offered it to Cassandra. Usually she was a wine person, but today she chose to embrace the moment and be one of the gang, clinking her glass with Terrance's before taking a refreshing sip of the cold, light ale.

Before fully engaging in any conversations, Cassandra took a moment to soak in the atmosphere of the hometown bar. The walls served as a testament to the town's pride and passion, adorned with framed jerseys, trophies, and signed photographs representing the local Carson High School and the legendary Huskers. Among the tapestry of nostalgia, a prominent banner near the pool tables paid homage to the Morton College Maples.

Cinda's husband, Jacob, and Meg's husband, Connor, had joined the group, their eyes glued to the basketball game while engaging in a side conversation with Fischer. Meanwhile, Gia chatted with Meg and

Shannon, while Simon Harris raised his glass in the air, acknowledging Cassandra with a nod and a silent "thanks."

They'd probably be arguing about something else soon, so she wanted to savor this moment of contentment amidst the recent tragedy. Moving to a small town had been a huge gamble, but she was doing it. This scene was what she had wanted for her new life without actually knowing it ahead of time. Not the part about hanging out in a loud bar with peanut shells and a few beer spills on the floor. The longing she'd felt was for community, a new *ohana*.

Across the table, Andy said, "Another case closed. Let's finish out the semester with a few weeks of mind-numbing boredom. No mayhem, no drama."

"Absolutely," Cassandra agreed. "I'm so ready for boredom and leisure time. In fact, I even hired the pooper scooper company that Nate works for to clean up Murphy's backyard messes."

Andy said, "How much poo can one little dog leave behind, anyway?"

"It's gross," Cassandra said. "But hey, the pooper scooper company hires starving college students, so it's like a charitable act in disguise."

The words just passed her lips when a hush settled over the bar. All eyes turned to the doorway where Chairman of the Board Alan Hershey appeared, blinking his eyes to adjust to the indoor lighting. With a casual air, artfully sculpted hair, and a polo shirt that screamed *I'm-casual-but-still-rich*, Alan made his way to their table.

Cassandra scooted her chair over to make room for him, as he accepted a beer from Connor before settling down next to her.

"Don't look so surprised, Cassandra," Hershey chuckled. "I'm no stranger to this dive. My daddy used to bring me here as a kid for Wednesday night Reubens and the occasional Sunday football pot roast. I was a farm kid who detasseled corn and walked beans, just like everyone in my class at school."

Cassandra was taken aback by his revelation. "Sorry," she couldn't hide her astonishment, her expression an open book. "I really should work on my poker face. I'm happy you're here. We're just celebrating the new president, and counting down the weeks until the semester's end." And now, she was intrigued by how little she knew about Hershey's background and roots in Carson.

"I overheard your conversations at the end of the committee meeting and decided to join you." He waited until a commercial break on the TV and stood. "I just wanted to congratulate y'all for your invaluable help this semester resolving some challenging situations. The students weren't the only ones who earned extra credit. You folks have been a great help to me personally in finding the right individual to lead Morton College. We look forward to welcoming Fran Morrison in the fall."

The group joined in a chorus of "Cheers!" as glasses clinked in celebration.

"Now that you'll have some free time, Alan," Jacob Weller said, "If you need help getting your boat in the water for some fishing this spring, you just let me know."

Simon, never one to miss an opportunity for humor, said, "Maybe now we'll see some real changes around here, starting with a free ice cream machine in the faculty lounge!"

Alan turned to Shannon and Cassandra. "Bob Soukup's going to be taking some time away from the board, so I wanted to inform you both that our next budget meeting in early April will include the matching funds for the emergency management system. I guarantee we won't lose that grant. Y'all have worked tirelessly to make this campus a better, safer place, and it's something we truly value."

Meg had been interpreting the toasts for Shannon, and when Hershey finished speaking, Shannon let out a "Whoop!" and raised his glass. He signed, *thank you!* They all cheered again, then the noise level in the bar returned to its previous level.

Shannon tapped his temple with a finger and signed to Cassandra, *Second intentions. It pays to think several steps down the road.*

Let's keep the swordfights to a minimum for awhile, please, she signed to him.

He typed on his phone for a short time, then handed it to her to read: IT'S SMART TO HAVE A PLAN. BUT LIFE'S UNPREDICTABLE, BE IT GOOD OR BAD. DON'T BE AFRAID TO TAKE RISKS, EVEN IF IT MEANS GOING AGAINST YOUR PLAN.

Confused by the unsolicited advice, she put her palms up like a half shrug. In reply, Shannon subtly dipped his head toward Fischer at the other end of the table. When Fischer turned and saw them both staring at him, he said, "What? Do I have ketchup on my chin?"

He wiped his face with a napkin while Cassandra shook her head and tried to hide her smirk. "Nothing. Shannon was just talking about fencing."

Fischer shrugged, and his gaze returned to the game.

"I appreciate you," Alan leaned in closer to Cassandra's ear. "I know it hasn't been easy for you here, but I hope you'll give Morton a chance. You've made a difference, and I believe there's more in store for you."

Cassandra's eyes welled up, momentarily clouding her vision. She hadn't realized how much her doubts had been visible to others. Gathering her thoughts, she told Alan, "I thought I knew what I wanted when I moved here. But Nebraska has surprised me. The students and the community make me feel like I belong."

As the night wore on, talk naturally shifted to summer plans. Meg said, "I'm kind of jealous of your study trip to Hawai'i this summer."

"You'll be too busy cuddling your bundle of joy to feel envious," Cassandra said. "Besides, leading a student trip to Oahu isn't exactly a beach vacation."

Amidst the laughter and celebration, Cassandra's mind circled back to the mystery that still nagged at her thoughts. Fischer and Fran's rendezvous at the field house tugged at her curiosity, fueling her desire for answers. She quietly confided in Meg, seeking advice and solace. "What if there's more to it? If nothing's going on, why can't he just tell me about their connection so I can move on?"

Meg squeezed Cassandra's hand reassuringly. "Connor has never said a negative word about Fischer, and I genuinely believe there's nothing for you to worry about. Trust in him, Cass."

"But—" Cassandra hesitated.

Connor leaned over Meg, "I ordered Meg some nachos. Do you need anything, Cass?"

"How about the power to see into the future?" She half-laughed. "Maybe ensure my boyfriend isn't about to make some colossal mistake with Morton's new president?"

Connor's handsome smile turned serious. His gaze flickered down the table to where Fischer sat, oblivious to their comments. "Sometimes it's better not to ask questions you don't want the answers to," Connor said, his voice serious. "But if you decide to delve deeper, be prepared for what you might find."

The night wound down, filled with laughter and hopeful anticipation. Cassandra felt a mixture of emotions—curiosity, determination, and a touch of apprehension—but she also embraced the boundless potential of the future that awaited her.

Book Club Discussion Guide

1. How does the author explore the theme of job interviews and hiring search committees in *Death 101: Extra Credit*? Did you find Cassandra's hiring experiences relatable or realistic?

2. Job interviews and job search committees can be highly competitive and stressful. Did you feel a connection to the characters' experiences? What was the most unusual job interview question you have been asked, or answers you have heard?

3. Discuss Cassandra Sato's actions in relation to her Deaf friend Shannon Bryant. How did her attempts to help him instead of allowing him to do things for himself affect their relationship? Did you sympathize with her intentions or question her choices?

4. Small towns often have a close-knit community where everyone knows each other's business. How does the author portray this aspect of small-town life in the book? Did it enhance or hinder the mystery plotline?

5. Scrabble game night at the neighbors plays a role in *Death 101: Extra Credit*. Did you have similar experiences in your own family? Share your favorite board games and any memorable moments you recall from your own game nights.

6. Explore the theme of letting go of a loved one in *Death 101: Extra Credit*. How does Cassandra's journey to move on from her fiancé Paul affect her character development? Did you find

her methods of coping relatable, and did they align with your own experiences or observations?

7. Loss of romantic or family relationships can have a profound impact on individuals. In the book, Cassandra writes a goodbye letter to Paul. How does this act of writing help her process her emotions and find closure? Have you ever used writing as a means of dealing with loss or grief?

8. Discuss the theme of finding purpose and fulfillment in one's current job in *Death 101: Extra Credit*. How does Cassandra's perspective on her role at Morton College evolve throughout the story? Did this theme resonate with you personally, and have you ever experienced a similar realization in your own career?

9. Cassandra initially sees her current job as a stepping stone to becoming a college president. However, she comes to understand the impact she can have on students at Morton College. Reflect on the significance of this realization. Have you ever had a similar shift in perspective regarding your own aspirations or goals? How did it affect your approach to your current situation?

10. The cozy mystery genre often combines elements of suspense and lightheartedness. How did *Death 101: Extra Credit* balance these two aspects? Did you find the mystery engaging, and were you able to solve it before the reveal?

Author Notes

High fives everyone! I feel like hosting a dance party to celebrate finishing *Death 101*. I want to thank so many people who made it possible:

Kristian Anderson, champion fencer and former *Three Musketeers* actor. His experience, knowledge, and creativity were pivotal in planting the seeds of this story and giving the fight scenes authenticity. Any technical errors are mine alone.

Lori Fairchild, my editor, friend, and gentle taskmaster.

My SCBWI critique group: Judith Snyder, Rosalind Reloj, Betty VanDeventer, and Boni Hamilton for pushing me outside my comfort zone.

A huge thanks as well to all of my morning writing sprint friends in the Cozy Mystery author community - you know who you are! I couldn't have finished this without your support. Special friends Lori Ideta and Auntie Evelyn Ideta, Crystal Ferry, Laura Chapman, Tosca Lee, Jayme Sandberg, Fr. Evan Winter, Thomas Beyer, and Jeff Walker. Also my Read it or Not Book Club and PPH members.

My husband Dave for taking on nearly all the household chores and the bulk of moving and packing duties as I raced to the finish line. Sipping cocktails in our new sunroom is my favorite new spot.

And last but not least, a giant hug goes out to my chief cheerleader and tireless first reader, Mom. Plus extra thanks to Dad, Sherri Brakenhoff, and Abbey Andress for being such expert proofreaders.

Huge thanks to my readers who kept the faith through a global pandemic, two children's books, and the longest wait ever for this story. It took two years of procrastination and many distractions, but hurray - here we are!

Thank you to everyone who supported the Kickstarter project to bring this book to publication faster and spread the word about the Cassandra Sato series to a wider audience.

Death 101 is based on actual college courses offered today, and an important part of this book's plotline. Though students won't get extra credit points for solving mysteries, they'll get an education like no other. If your university offers something similar, I recommend taking it without hesitation.

About the Author

photo credit: Susan Noel

Kelly Brakenhoff is an American Sign Language Interpreter whose motivation for learning ASL began in high school when she wanted to converse with her Deaf friends. She divides her writing time between the Cassandra Sato Mystery Series and a children's book series featuring Duke the Deaf Dog. A wife, mother of four young adults and a hunting dog, and proud grandma, Kelly and her husband call Nebraska home.

Sign up for monthly emails with Kelly's special offers, recipes, and book recommendations here:

https://brakenville.myflodesk.com/dbydend

Reach Kelly at her website at kellybrakenhoff.com

Get the latest updates on Facebook: https://www.facebook.com/kellybrakenhoffauthor/

www.ingramcontent.com/pod-product-compliance
Lightning Source LLC
Chambersburg PA
CBHW061445210726
48287CB00007B/2364